KILLER

COIREE GUARDIANS

BOOK TWO

MARI MINIATT

Tiff ~~thanks~~ Thanks for coming
Mari M.

ANIMATED LIAR MEDIA

This is a work of fiction. Names, characters, businesses, places, events and incidents are either the products of the author's imagination or used in a fictitious manner. Any resemblance to actual persons, living or dead, or actual events is purely coincidental

Printed in the United States of America

First Printing, 2010

ISBN 978-0-9826660-2-9

Animated Lair Media

Syracuse, NY

Book design and production by Animated Liar Media

Editing by Animated Liar Media and Josh Shear.

Dedication

There are many people I want to thank that help make this book a reality:

My husband and boys, for being understanding.

The staff at the Enchanted Bazaar, and all the great people I meet there. If I need a charge I know where to go.

Veronica for being one of the first people to hear about these characters and pushing me on.

Jeremiah you gave me such a great writing challenge you are now immortalized in this book.

All the people in person and online that gave me advice and critiques.

Thanks to all of you.

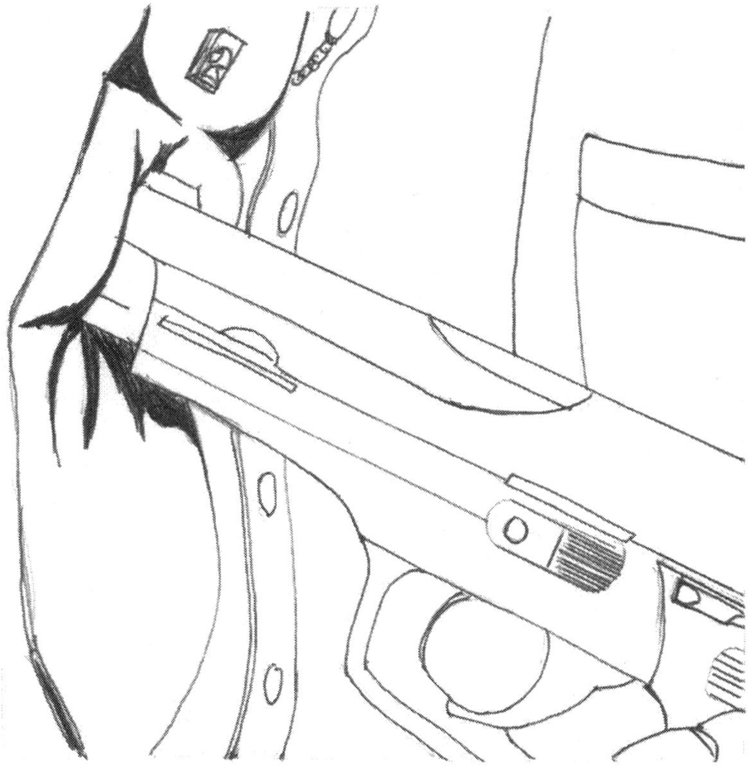

CHAPTER 1

The blood flowed like molasses away from the body. It laid across the back hallway, limp, lifeless, and headless. Swen shook his head, his cheeks turning red under his beard. Vincent nudged the unattached head closer to the body.

"Sorry, man," Vincent said, handing Swen a rag.

Swen took the rag with a sharp flick of his wrist. "If you were to spray this place down with luminol it would glow like a goddamn disco."

"It was a slaughterhouse," Vincent said. He shook the spray bottle.

"You're the slaughterhouse." Swen blotted the blood on the wall.

"Who was this?"
"Huh?"
Swen motioned with his head toward the dead body. A dripping noise started at a slow rhythm, then sped up to a steady stream. The blood trickled down the grate.
"Small-time drug dealer." Vincent fingered the bullet hole in his vest. "Asshole shot me."
Swen grabbed the spray bottle. "I took care of the last one."
"I know, I know." Vincent stood up. "Don't worry, I'll get this place clean before the band shows. Where is the pressure washer?"
Swen pointed to the body. "Take care of that, first."
Vincent walked over to a large grate set in the floor. The grate had been one of the original parts of the slaughterhouse. The cast iron was twisted into ornate shapes that were too fancy for its purpose. He pulled it out as easy as pulling out a drawer. He kicked the body down the hole, threw the head down, then replaced the grate.
"Done."
Swen flung back his long ponytail and stood up. "Lorelei is gonna kill you."
"He tried to kill me."
"Like he could have."
Lorelei came down the hallway, she stopped. She placed one hand on her hip and the other she pointed at Vincent. "What the hell?" Her finger hitting the air with each word.
"It was a drug dealer."
Swen took out his pocket knife. "Oh, look, there's the bullet." He used his knife to dig the bullet out the drywall.
"He shot you?" Lorelei came closer. She put her hands on Vincent's shoulder and turned him around. "You should change."
"Why?"
"It ripped up your back."
"Dammit."
Swen slapped the bullet in Vincent's hand. "You better hold on to that."
"Thanks."
"Where should I tell Grady to look for this one?" Swen asked, motioning with his head to the grating.
"I don't know yet." Vincent said.

“At least we can block this off,” Lorelei said. “We finally get a full house this season and you have to play guillotine.”

“It's not-”

She held up her hand. “Just change. I would throw that silk shirt out. It's ruined.”

Vincent ran upstairs and changed his clothes. When he got back down, he could hear Swen running the power washer. He walked into the main floor of the Burgundy Rathskeller and smiled.

All the tables that usually sat in the middle of the floor had been moved into the back store room. The only seating left for the night was the permanent booths along the walls. The candelabras had been moved up into the ceiling and secured. The place looked ready for the band.

Lorelei had her cell phone hooked between her shoulder and ear. Her red and blue hair matched the custom case on the phone. She laid a tray of clean glasses on the counter and started to line them up under the bar as she spoke.

“Are you sure?” she asked.

She stopped and reached for a pad of paper and a pencil. After taking down some notes, she motioned to Vincent with her thumbs up. She put her phone down. “We're sold out.”

“That's probably why that guy was hanging around,” Vincent said. He walked to the bar. “I went outside to make sure the parking spaces were saved for the bus, and he hits me up to buy some coke.”

“His first mistake was thinking you were a coke head,” Lorelei said.

She looked around the bar, moving a few items, then she disappeared behind the bar. Vincent glanced at the clock; the rest of the staff should be here soon. Lorelei popped back up. She leaned on the bar, flipping open a notebook.

“Could you take this list and make sure it's all in the lounge?” she asked. She ripped a piece of paper out of the notebook.

Vincent took the paper. It listed almost every type of alcohol they carried at the bar. He grabbed a cart from the back hallway and unlocked the liquor store room. The band had ordered the typical assortment of wines, whiskey, and vodka. Someone had requested hot pepper schnapps. He would have to give the cleaning crew a bonus after tonight.

As he loaded up the cart, the bar became quieter. He could hear Swen cursing and the sounds of a hose hitting the wall. Vincent had most of the bottles loaded when Swen walked by, pulling the power washer. He shook his finger at Vincent.

"No more bodies tonight, all right?"

"I can't promise," Vincent said, but he flashed Swen a grin.

Swen snorted. He flung the hose over his shoulder and continued down the hall. Vincent double-checked the list, then left the store room.

In the lounge, Vincent pushed the cart of alcohol in as John sat down a platter of food. His dredlocks held back in a thick, short ponytail. He pushed up his glasses when Vincent entered. "Hey, you gonna help?"

Vincent held up the piece of paper. "Lorelei wants me to double-check."

John chuckled. "Good, you got the booze."

He pulled another platter of food out from the tall metal rack. He unwrapped it as Vincent loaded up the mini bar in the lounge.

"At least this band eats healthy," John said.

Vincent glanced at the table. There were sandwiches, fruit, two platters of vegetables. He then looked at the list in his hand. "Except they drink shit."

John took the list and then shook his head. "No taste." He handed the list back. "I'm missing the mixed drinks."

"I'll get them," Vincent said.

He went back out to the bar. Andi had just come in. She was wearing a t-shirt that had a single rose bud coming out of a pool of blood.

"Hey!" she said, smiling. Her ponytails glowed blue in the lights behind the bar.

"That is a nice shirt," Vincent said.

"Janice let me borrow it." Andi stuck out her chest. "She says it accents my tits."

Vincent laughed. Andi pulled the shirt down. She shrugged. "I don't know about that, these get noticed no matter what I wear."

"Those are why you get the tips."

"And I thought it was my great personality."

Vincent handed her the list. "Can you take care of this list for me?"

Lorelei walked by, arguing a point in the contract with someone on the other end of her phone. She waved to Vincent, then covered the cell phone with her free hand.

"The band is pulling up now!"

Vincent motioned with his hands. "I'll go."

He went to the side door and opened it. A couple of roadies gave him thankful looks. They picked up some of the equipment and dragged it in, knocking the snow off as they came inside. Vincent stood by the door, giving directions.

He watched the traffic on the street when he wasn't helping move something over the door jamb or telling people where to go. The snow had stopped earlier in the day and the temperature had dropped. The roadies hurried inside, moving as fast as they could to get out of the cold. Their steaming breaths would continue inside the club as the wind whipped into the open door.

The band's bus pulled up on the side street and parked. Vincent felt something. He pretended to rub his hands in the cold and walked toward the bus. As he got closer, the feeling got stronger. He stopped at the door of the bus and smiled. On that bus was a vampire that he knew.

Vincent walked back to the club, swinging his arms and whistling. He went to the bar. Lorelei glanced in his direction, then turned her attention back to the road manager. Vincent walked behind the bar and poured a large brandy. He swirled the drink in the glass. Lorelei pushed her blue hair behind her ear and gave Vincent a strange look.

The band shuffled in a few moments later. Vincent put the brandy on a tray. He found a lighter behind the bar and placed it near the brandy. He picked up the tray, balancing it on his fingers, then he went to the lounge and knocked.

A large man in a security shirt opened the door, he stepped aside and allowed Vincent to enter. He found the other vampire. She sat on the couch next to a couple of members of the band. She smiled when she saw Vincent.

Her long fingers curled around a black cigarette holder, the cigarette dangled a long ash at the other end. Even with her dark hair up, it still looked wild. Vincent set the tray down in front of her.

"Oh my god," she said. Her voice had a hint of an Italian accent.

"Vincent!"

"Verina!"

She stood up, her already tall stature accented by the high heeled boots she wore. The man that had been sitting next to her looked up. He gave Vincent a dirty look.

Verina leaned over and hugged Vincent. Then she kissed him on both cheeks. Vincent picked up the brandy. "How ya doing?"

"Good," she said. She motioned to the lead singer. "Toby, this is an old friend of mine. Vincent."

Toby sneered at the words "old friend." Verina rolled her eyes and took a long drag of her cigarette. Vincent handed her the brandy. She blew the smoke out over the glass.

Vincent smiled at Toby. "You guys got everything?"

"A couple of white Russians," the bald man sitting next to Toby said.

"I'll go see how they're coming." Vincent winked at Verina. Toby's eyes narrowed.

She took a long drag off her cigarette. *Yeah, I know.* Her voice sounded clear in Vincent's head. *He's a bit jealous.*

"Nice seeing you, Verina."

Vincent went back to the bar to make the drinks. *So, another musician?* Vincent asked Verina.

I'm a sucker for them, I know. You're going to see more of me.

Really, why? Vincent mixed the drinks.

Toby is composing the music for a movie being filmed in town. The producers want him around for the whole filming.

Vincent walked back to the room. *What movie is this?* he asked.

Ashes at Dawn.

Vincent opened the door and placed the drinks in front of the bald man. He thanked Vincent as he spun a drumstick in his left hand. Verina now reclined against Toby on the couch. Toby wrapped his arms around her. She kissed his cheek.

"Hope you have a good show," Vincent said. He left the room, trying not to laugh.

A few hours later they opened the doors. Swen and three other men worked the front. Vincent wandered into the bouncer booth to watch the mass of people come inside. Even with the horrible cold outside the club filled. Swen closed the doors after the last of them filed in. He blew on his hands.

"Good crowd," he said.

The opening act started their set. Vincent sat in the bouncer booth with Swen, bullshitting. When the main band went on, Vincent excused himself and went to the back of the club. The normal collection of people that always hung out during the shows filled the back hallway. Vincent weaved his way through friends of the band, groupies, music promoters, a disc jockey from the local radio station, and the roadies.

He found Verina still sitting in the lounge. A group of women stood on the other side of the room. They would look at Verina with a mixture of jealousy and envy in their eyes. Vincent walked in. Verina waved.

"Why aren't you watching Toby?" Vincent asked.

Verina shrugged. "I've seen it." She stood up, pulling down her leather skirt at the same time. "I need some air."

"I got a great place, come on."

Verina followed Vincent up to the roof of the club. They stood on top of the Rathskeller. Neither of them wore jackets. Verina only had on her leather skirt and blouse. The wind blew across the top of the roof, making the vents shake with its force. The sounds of the concert could only be heard when the wind didn't blow.

"You look good," Vincent said.

"Thanks."

"That look is an improvement. Last time I saw you, you wore a beret and a black turtleneck."

"But I could smoke anywhere." Verina lit a cigarette.

Vincent shook his head. Verina glanced at the cigarette in her hand. "It's not going to kill me."

She took a long drag and walked to the edge of the roof. "I still can't believe you live here."

"Either here or in Forest Grove."

Verina ran her fingers through her hair. Her fingernails glinted in the lights from the street lamps. "Don't get me wrong. It's a nice club."

"You and Toby..."

Verina smirked. "He likes it. I think he gets off when I feed from him."

"Ah."

"What's your deal here?" Verina asked. "That cute waitress?"

"Actually, I have a few people. I made a deal with two of them. They feed me, I gave them this building."

"That's nice," Verina said.

"How long are you sticking around Toby?"

"His band is taking off. I have a lot of fun so far. So I stay." The wind blew her hair around her head. "I'll stick around for a little while longer."

"Anyone say anything?"

Verina shook her head. "The rest of the band thinks we are just a weird couple. What have you been up to?"

Vincent leaned on the cinder block. "Nothing much. Help run the club. Oh, yeah, my donor, John, his sister became a vampire. I would have helped her out a lot more, but she is linked to this other vampire and adjusted very fast."

"None of that 'I can't drink blood' bullshit?" Verina asked.

"Nope."

"Good." Verina smiled. "Too many now-a-days want it like it's in the books. I say have fun being a ghoul."

Vincent laughed.

Verina finished her cigarette. "I'll talk to Toby. He doesn't realize that you are like me. When he does, he'll lighten up."

"It's not that important." Vincent said.

"It is to me," Verina said. She placed her hand on his shoulder. "You know I have always considered you my baby brother."

"I know."

"Even though my real baby brother was a tyrant."

"One of these days you are going to have to explain that to me."

The crowd went wild downstairs. Verina shook the snow off her hair and shoulders. "We should go."

She turned to walk toward the entrance to the attic. Vincent got an idea. "Hey, Verina, do you want to see the old place?"

Verina stopped. "It still stands?"

Vincent nodded.

Verina didn't smile, but she nodded. "It would be interesting."

They went back downstairs. The band played an encore. Verina stood beside Vincent at the bar for a few moments. When it sounded as if the band was hitting the last chorus. Verina waved to Vincent.

She walked through the crowd without having to push her way

through. The crowd would open up around her as she walked to the back of the club. Vincent glanced over his shoulder. Lorelei watched Verina, then looked at him.

"Who was that?" She shouted.

"What?" Vincent shouted.

"That woman?"

"An old friend."

"I like her boots," Lorelei said.

Vincent chuckled. She crossed her arms and gave him a dirty look.

"What?"

"Don't you have a mess to clean up?" She pointed to the floor.

"I'll get to it."

Lorelei went back to tending the bar. Vincent pulled the keys out of his pocket. Andi came around the corner. She spun around to avoid hitting Vincent. He wrapped his hands around her waist.

"Want to help me with another job?" he asked.

"If it's anything to do with that dead body, gross, no."

"How did you know?"

"Lorelei told me," Andi said. She tugged at his goatee. "See you later."

Vincent let her go. He went into the back room of the bar. John sat in the office. He chuckled as Vincent passed by. Vincent stopped.

"What?"

"Andi likes flirting with you."

"She knows it's not going anywhere."

"What about those other women?"

Vincent grinned. "I just leave them with some good memories."

"Good, I don't think we could keep cleaning the mess up."

Vincent shook the keys in his hand. "I'm going."

That's one advantage to using donors, Vincent thought. No more messes. But no hunting, either.

He opened the back door. The wind whipped through the alleyway. He paused as he put the key in the lock. He looked at his claws and smiled. It had been fun taking that dealer's head off. He chuckled as he went into the basement. The wind blew, drowning out his laughter.

CHAPTER 2

Two nights later, Vincent glanced over the half-full club looking for the right one. He saw a tall blond talking to a middle-aged man in a business suit. Vincent touched her mind; too materialistic. Nothing on her mind but sports cars and clothes. Across the room a dark-haired woman sat along the wall. She had vile thoughts in her head for someone named Jack.

He saw her. A cute redhead wearing a tight corset that showed off all the curves she had. He felt her mind and found what she wanted to drink. She liked fuzzy navels. Vincent went behind the bar to mix her one. Good taste was not what he was looking for right now.

He walked over to the table and set the drink down in front of the redhead. He already knew her name. “Sandra, someone sent this over.”

“Really? Who?” Sandra said, scanning the crowd.

“Me.”

Sandra locked her pretty green eyes on him. “You?”

Vincent smiled.

She pointed to his fangs. “Those look real.”

“They are real,” he said.

“Right,” a dark-haired girl said. “I suppose you are going to tell us you are five hundred years old.”

“What's your name?” Vincent asked.

“Terri.”

“A century and a half, maybe. Terri.”

Terri gave him a dirty look. She sat back in the booth and turned her face away. The other three girls all adjusted their posture so they showed more cleavage. Sandra giggled again.

Vincent found a few interesting things in her mind. She liked his fangs, but wished they were longer. The name Stephan kept bubbling to the surface. He touched the minds of the three girls; he left Terri alone. She had made it clear that she didn't want his attention. The other three girls also thought about some man named Stephan.

Vincent sat down at the booth, sliding in so he could sit next to Sandra. She blushed. Vincent picked a hair off her shoulder. Sandra leaned close to him. He could smell her perfume, a sweet mixture of roses and jasmine.

“Come here often?” she asked. The three girls laughed. Terri glared.

“I work here.”

“What do you do?”

“Find the prettiest girls and make sure they have a good time.” Vincent moved Sandra's drink closer to her. “I think you need to have a good time.”

Sandra's eyes went wide. She laughed. “It's just like in 'Flower Ashes,' when Bianca met Stephan at the club.”

Every woman at the table nodded but Terri. Sandra stroked Vincent's goatee. “Are you like Stephan?” she asked.

“Depends,” Vincent said. “Is he a good dancer?”

Sandra giggled.

Vincent stood up. “You want to find out?”

He held out his hand. Sandra took it, giggling. He led her out to the dance floor. She wouldn't stop giggling. Vincent brushed her hair back as they started to dance.

Stop giggling, he thought.

Her giggling ceased. Vincent pulled her closer. She glanced over her shoulder and smiled at her friends. Vincent caught a look from John in the DJ cage. He rolled his eyes. Vincent guided Sandra across the floor, closer to the hallway that led to his private room.

That name Stephan kept coming to her mind. Vincent could not get a good image of him. But he could sense that Sandra found just the idea of that man exciting.

She danced closer to him. He stroked her neck. She shivered. Vincent ran the tip of his fangs across her neck. She melted. He had to grasp her waist to keep her from falling.

Sandra whispered in his ear. “They feel real.”

He moved her closer to the hallway. At the end of the song, he dipped her. She giggled. He spun her around and down the hallway to his private room. He wrapped his arm around her waist. “Come into my parlor?”

Sandra's eyes unfocused. “Are you a spider?”

Vincent smiled, forcing his fangs out longer. Sandra shivered. “Those are real?”

He unlocked the door and pushed it open. Sandra turned around and opened her mouth in surprise. “Wow, it's...”

“It's just a room.”

The room had a fainting couch, a low coffee table, and heavy wood paneling. The paneling covered the sound barrier along the walls. The barrier had been put up to keep the sounds of the club out of the room. But sometimes things went wrong and Vincent did not want the club to hear the screams from inside.

Sandra sat down on the fainting couch looking around the room with wide unfocused eyes. Vincent lit the large pillar candle next to the couch and turned off the lights. He sat down beside her.

“What brought you to my club tonight?” Vincent asked her, running his fingers down the lacing of her corset.

“We thought it would be a lark to come to a goth club, we never have before,” Sandra said.

"Are you having a good time?"

Sandra nodded. Vincent leaned close to her face and whispered in her ear. "We could have more fun."

She shuddered. Vincent touched her mind again. She had a vivid imagination. He would not have to put any ideas in her head. He kissed her. Kissing meant nothing to him. It was only part of the process. Sandra kissed him back with such eagerness that Vincent almost pushed her away. Instead he lifted his lips to her ears.

"Lay back," he said.

Sandra did. She stretched herself over the fainting couch and on his lap. Vincent undid the laces on her corset. He ran his fingers under her breasts.

She inhaled a brisk breath through her teeth. "Your fingers are cold," she said.

"Of course they are," he said. He brushed his lips on her neck then whispered in her ear. "Close your eyes."

She closed her eyes. He sat back and waited. She moaned. He brushed her hair away from her neck. As he leaned in, Sandra slid her hand down and pulled up her white skirt. Vincent pulled down her necklace. Sandra moaned again.

He whispered, "No pain."

Vincent bit her neck. She gasped and pulled him closer. She moved her hips as if they were having sex. Vincent clasped one arm around her so she did not fall off the couch. He pulled his lips off her neck after he had drank his fill. Her body still reacted to the sex they were not having. Vincent watched her. She moaned.

When her moaning ended, Vincent whispered, "That was nice."

Sandra opened her eyes. She couldn't focus on Vincent.

"It was a good time, right?" he asked.

She smiled. Her eyes focused on him. He pulled her skirt down. "I've never done that before," she said.

"There is always a first time," he said. He kissed her, this time on the forehead. As he did, he put an idea in her head. *You have to leave. You forgot to feed your pet.* Vincent ran his fingers along her neck where he had bitten her. Her neck looked like it had when they came into room. Not even a red mark.

Sandra blushed and sat up. "Oh my god. I have to go home. I hope you understand."

Vincent nodded. "I do."

She stood up, tying her corset.

"Wait." Vincent pulled out a blank card from his wallet. He handed it to Sandra. "My number."

She took the card and read it. In her mind she saw his name and number. Vincent made sure she did. She smiled and ran out of the room. He stood up and checked the couch. Not a drop had fallen on it. He adjusted the pillows, brushed off the cushion, and blew out the candle. He sat on the couch and waited a few minutes.

When he left his private room. All of Sandra's friends had left the table except for Terri. Vincent nodded toward her. Terri smiled, but it wasn't a friendly one. He passed by the other girls on the dance floor.

Terri marched over to Vincent. "What did you do to Sandra?"

"Nothing."

"She took off."

"She told me she had to get home."

"What?"

Vincent sighed. He forced his mind into hers. *Her pet is hungry.* He thought.

Terri's face softened. "Oh, she forgot..."

She blushed and went back to the table. Vincent continued to the back of the club. He saw himself behind the bar in the video monitors that took the place of the traditional mirrors. Lorelei stood to the side of the bar, sipping a soda. He patted her on the shoulder as he passed by.

He leaned against the door frame to the office. Inside, Andi sat with her feet up at the desk. She had a book on her lap and held a sandwich in one hand. She didn't look up from her book, but waved to Vincent.

"Break time?" Vincent asked.

Andi nodded and swallowed. "Lunch." She turned a page. "I can't believe Janice convinced me to read this."

"Bad?" Vincent asked.

Andi put the book down. "Not the worst thing I read, not really my type of story. I never liked romance."

Vincent sat down next to the desk. "*Wuthering Heights* was pretty good."

"I didn't like *Wuthering Heights,* either. And believe me, this is not even close to it."

Vincent glanced at the book. The painting on the cover was a typical romance pose. A man holding a woman close to him while the wind blew their clothing. Vincent shook his head. He never understood romances.

Andi finished her food. She balled up the sandwich paper and threw it in the garbage, raising her hands in victory when it went into the can. Vincent pushed the book toward her.

"Why don't you read me some?" he asked.

"No." Andi got out of her seat. She stood behind Vincent and rubbed his shoulders.

"You don't have to do that," he said.

Andi sighed.

"What is it?"

"Nothing." She took her hands off his shoulders.

"Andi," Vincent said. "You only give me back rubs when you are upset."

"I'm not upset. I just have a lot on my mind."

"What is it?"

"There is a movie coming to town. I want to be an extra," Andi said. "Anyway, the tryouts are tomorrow and I'm nervous."

Vincent reached back and gave her a hug. "It's just an extra. You will do fine."

John walked into the office. "Is this a group hug?"

Vincent dropped his arms and Andi laughed. John fingered his way through a drawer in the CD cabinet. Vincent put his feet up on the desk. Andi sat down on his lap. She picked up the book. It had covered a large envelope on the desk.

Vincent picked up the envelope.

"Lorelei wanted to talk to you about it," John said.

"What is it?"

"A contract to use the Rathskeller for a movie." John placed the pile of CDs in the crook of his arm.

"A movie?"

"Yeah, *Ashes at Dawn*."

"I heard that title before," Vincent said.

Andi held the cover of the book in Vincent's face. He read the title, ignoring the semi-naked couple on the cover. "*Ashes at Dawn*, I see. Seems to be a popular subject lately."

"It's a popular series," Andi said. "All my roommates have read it. One of them thinks the author, Nathan Stout, is a real vampire, and one even got Stephan's name tattooed on her leg."

John shook his head. "That was stupid. I tell people I won't do their favorite bands, books, or movies unless they have another reason, like they screwed the singer or something."

"I know. I tried to convince her not to get it," Andi said.

"Stephan?" Vincent chuckled. "I see."

"The filming would be a good idea," John said. "They do have a good compensation rate, and it would be kinda cool to see the club on the big screen."

Vincent put the envelope down. "Two problems. No one can go upstairs or in the basement."

"They will have to go in the basement, but only to the utility room," John said. "But the upstairs is off limits."

"Do you think it would be a good idea?" Vincent asked Andi.

"Just based on what my roommates will do when they find out the film is being shot here? Hell! Yes!"

"What will they do?"

"After they are done screaming, and I get my hearing back, they'll camp out in front of this place."

"You're teasing me."

John shook his head. "She's not. One of the other nightclub owners came over today and offered us a couple of thousand to turn them down."

Vincent slid the envelope away from him on the desk. "Sounds good. I'll talk to Lorelei about it later."

Andi glanced at her watch. "Damn, back to the grind."

She jumped off his lap. On her way out the door she blew Vincent a kiss.

John slammed the drawer shut. "What is going to happen when she finds someone?"

"Same thing I did when you and Lorelei started to date. Nothing."

John pointed to the envelope. "I'll tell Lorelei you'll get with her."

"Thanks."

John balanced the CDs on his arm as he left the office. Vincent picked up *Ashes at Dawn* and read the book's jacket.

"Stephan Ashington has been on this world for over two hundred years. He doesn't find life again until he meets Angelica. Her love is what his undead heart needs."

Vincent shook his head. "Poor baby. You're going to disappoint her in bed."

He ran his fingers through his hair and leaned back on the chair. What was it with humans? When he became a vampire, he was a monster. He would get his victims alone and they would scream if he gave them a chance. But now? They wanted a candlelight dinner before he could have his meal.

He turned his attention to the security monitors. He watched Swen walk across the main floor. Andi stood next to a table full of young men, taking their orders. Swen came into the office. He changed the battery in his walkie talkie. Vincent held up the book.

"What do you think of this?" Vincent asked.

Swen glanced at the book. "I like Zane Grey."

"Is this really what people think of when they think of vampires?" Vincent asked.

Swen shrugged. "Anything wrong with it?"

"Makes feeding easier," Vincent said. "But I don't know..."

"So what?"

Vincent shook his head and made himself sigh. "Performance anxiety?"

"What?"

"I haven't been able to get it up since 1888."

"I did not need to know that," Swen said, laughing.

"No biggie, I don't worry about it."

"What if you met a real cutie?" Swen asked.

"Nothing. She would be fun to look at, but nothing."

"Too bad, man."

"Well, we don't need to reproduce that way."

"Like I said, too bad." Swen saluted Vincent and left the office. Vincent watched Swen weave his way through the crowd on the monitor. I have it good, he thought. I don't need to hunt every night.

Static came over the speaker of a walkie talkie sitting in the charger.

"Dance floor, back booths," Swen said over the speaker.

Vincent hurried out to the dance floor. A drunk man grabbed Andi. She pushed him back.

“Sit down,” she said. “I will have to call security.”

“You got nice tits,” he said. He made another grab for her. He got the tips of his fingers into the top of her corset. Andi tensed. Vincent stopped. Swen at the other side of the dance floor did the same.

Andi's face turned red. She threw down the drink tray. The glasses breaking, splattering drinks across the nearby tables, the customers jumping and squealing at the sudden rain of alcohol. Andi threw one punch, then the kicks flew. She moved fast, so fast the kicks seemed to come out of nowhere. Andi aimed each strike with such precision and speed, the drunk crumbled to the floor after five blows.

“Why'd you do that, bitch?” The drunk sobbed.

Andi bent down and picked up her tray, as Swen approached.

“You okay?” Swen asked.

“No, I'm not,” the drunk said.

“I'm not talking to you,” Swen said, picking the drunk up by the shirt collar. “You're going out.”

Vincent bent down to help Andi. He threw some pieces of the broken glasses on Andi's tray. She bent down, her face still red. She pressed her lips together until they turned white. Vincent placed his hand on her arm. “You all right?”

Andi nodded.

“Next time warn people you are an expert Savateuse,” Vincent said.

“Like he would have known what that is,” Andi sighed. “I got to get back to work.”

She picked up the tray and glared at the other men sitting at the table.

“Is she a ninja or something?” one of the men at the table asked after she left.

“Kick-boxing,” Vincent said. “You saw our bouncer. She knocked him down until he was crying.”

The men glanced at each other. One of them stood up. “I'll go see if he needs a ride.”

Vincent pointed his finger at the rest of the men. He let the tip of his finger turn into a claw. “No touching the wait staff, alright?”

Instead of responding, all of them bowed their heads and became interested in their drinks. Vincent walked away.

He found a secluded spot near the hallway to his room. Terri and the rest of Sandra's friends were leaving the club. Lorelei stood with her arm around Andi's shoulder, behind the bar. Andi nodded at something Lorelei said.

Then he watched the crowd. When they had first opened the Rathskeller, their main customers would spend hours on their costumes. Everyone tried to look different. Not anymore.

Two men walked by him, both dyed their hair black and wore fake fangs. The fake fangs were easy to spot: they would glow in the black lights that lined the walls. The men's clothing had the name of the shop where they had bought it embroidered across the pockets. A third man joined them. He had painted his face with white and black makeup.

Most of the women wore the same outfit: short skirt and corset. One woman did try for something different. She sat in a booth across from Vincent, dressed in a full mourning costume. The large hat, the veil, and dress, all in black lace. She laughed, her fangs glowed.

Vincent closed his eyes for a moment. The last fight he had with another vampire had been when Rebecka had turned. He could not remember the last time he went out on a hunt. He hit the back of his head against the wall.

"I need to get out more."

CHAPTER 3

Lorelei walked downstairs with Vincent after he had his meal. “I was hoping you would be okay with the offer from the film company,” she said.

“As long as they do not go upstairs, and Swen is with them in the basement.”

“I'm not an idiot.”

“I didn't say you were.”

“Right... Swen has a new guy.”

Vincent stopped. “We need another bouncer?”

“It's to help out while they are filming.” Lorelei flicked her green spikes of hair. “The crew says it won't be a problem; they brought their own security. But I have to have people here I can trust.”

“Good thinking.”

Lorelei got the spikes to stand up. “I have to do some paperwork. Catch you later.”

She went into the office. He continued on into the bar area. A young man stood alongside Swen, leaning against the bar. In front of them were sheets of papers. Swen had one in his hand. The young man looked normal. But Vincent could smell that this young man was not.

Swen looked up. “Vince, this is Chuck Navarro. He's gonna be helping out in security.”

Vincent held out his hand. Chuck shook it. He looked like he was in his mid-twenties, but his eyes looked older. Vincent noticed that both he and Chuck sniffed the air when they shook hands. He kept his face emotionless as he released his grip.

“Vincent is one of your bosses,” Swen said. “The only time you don't listen to him is if Lorelei overrides what he said.”

“You don't want a pissed-off Lorelei,” Vincent said.

Chuck stifled a laugh.

“I'm gonna have Chuck be my shadow for a few days. We need the help.”

“Ever done security before?” Vincent asked.

Chuck nodded, his shaggy hair cut shook, dropping his bangs over his eyes. He flung back his long bangs with his hand. “A couple of times, but not like this.”

“Most of the filming will be done during the day, so we won't be around much at night,” Swen said. “Cassie loves the idea of me sleeping at the same time she does.”

“Are they doing any filming at night?” Vincent asked.

“A few days' worth, mainly outside shots, I understand,” Swen said. “But you never know.”

Vincent smiled at Chuck. “I'm sure working here would be an eye opening experience.” He motioned with his head to Swen. “I need to go over something with you.”

“Sure. Chuck, why don't you go over the forms again, then wait for me in the cage, okay?”

Chuck nodded. He didn't have the build of any of the other

bouncers that Swen had hired. He seemed fragile. Vincent rubbed his hands. But Chuck had a strong handshake, almost as strong as Steopa's.

"Swen?" Vincent asked. He motioned to Chuck with his head.

"He's not a berserk," Swen said. "Whatever he is, he doesn't want me to know."

"Do you think he figured you out?" Vincent asked. "He could smell me."

Swen shook his head. "I'm confusing the hell out of him."

"Good." Vincent rubbed his beard. He looked around the empty club.

"You all right?" Swen asked.

"I think. I'm going out tonight. Tell Lorelei, all right?"

"Sure, gotta warn you, it snowed like a son of bitch earlier," Swen said.

"Thanks."

Vincent stopped on his way out the door and grabbed a jacket. He didn't need it, but people looked at him strange if he didn't wear one in the middle of winter. He walked up the ramp and out onto the snow-covered street.

Winter this year had already been brutal. It was late November and two blizzards had already shut Deerbow down. It felt like it was going to be cold and nasty for rest of the coming months. Vincent smiled at the tall piles of snow left by the plows. Winter is the best season for a vampire, he thought.

He glanced at a clock as he walked over the few inches of snow on the sidewalk. Seven pm, a time he only got to see when there was white on the ground. The streets were not empty. The people who lived in this city were used to snow and wind and dropping temperatures, so a few inches of snow wasn't going to stop them.

Vincent watched a couple hurry from their cab to a restaurant. A beggar tried to stop them on their way in, but they ignored him. Vincent chuckled. The two blizzards had sent some of the beggars running to warmer climes, but a few always tried to stick it out.

He recognized the part of town he walked in. When he was human, this was the factory section. The blue collar part of town. The place Vincent spent most of his adulthood. The bars he had passed out in were long gone. Most of the old factory buildings had been torn down or made into condos.

Now it was for the young professionals. The ones with money but nothing to spend it on, but themselves. This time of night would be busy, but not busy enough to justify the line Vincent saw forming down the street. He crossed to the other side of the street and walked passed the line.

He stopped in front of a coffee shop and tried to figure out what was happening. Women made up most of the line. He could see young women and old women standing together talking. The conversations were fluttering around like butterflies full of excitement. The only people in the line who did not join in were the few men.

Vincent found the front of the line. It started at a bookstore. A large poster had been put out. 'One night only! Author Nathan Stout! Ashes Rekindled! Midnight!' Vincent chuckled. He had not seen a line like that for a writer since Mark Twain.

Past the new development in the old part of town, Vincent came to a part of town that had been left to rot. He sensed two vampires nearby. He turned into the direction he which felt them.

The path led to an old park that the city had not bothered to fix up in decades. It had been taken over by vandals. He walked over a bridge that had so much graffiti on it that the original color was anyone's guess. He came to a crest of a hill looking down to the lower level of the park. A young man raced across the open ground.

He had his head turned, watching for what was behind him. Vincent could hear his heartbeats from where he was standing. They sounded as if he was playing a drum solo with his heart.

Vincent faded into the shadows and watched. The two other shapes blurred by. The olive green blur almost over took the running man. The darker blur got ahead of him and stopped. The dark blur coalesced. It was Rebecka. She clotheslined the man. His head snapped back and he fell into the green blur. The green blur turned into the giant Steopa.

Vincent waited until they had fed off their victim. Steopa stood up, his giant frame becoming another long shadow on the ground. Rebecka stepped over the body and wrapped her arms around Steopa. Vincent jumped off the bridge, landing on top of the deep snow beneath it, not leaving any footprints on the dirty white ground.

"Vincent!" Rebecka ran to him and gave him a hug. "It's great to see you."

Vincent stepped back and looked at Rebecka, she seemed taller now. She did not have the hunched, beaten look about her, like she did when she was alive. He noticed a red ring on her finger. She had started to wear that after she became a vampire. But this was the first time Vincent saw it glowing. The dull red glow of the ring took attention away from her long blue coat, which made her look like a quilted blueberry.

Steopa walked over, buttoning up his greatcoat. He still wore the Russian officer's long coat. Vincent tried not to grin when he saw the fur hat on Steopa's head. If there wasn't a billboard behind him advertising a trip to Las Vegas, Vincent could have sworn he ended up in Siberia.

"Cold night to be out," Steopa said. His Slavic accent had gotten a little softer.

Vincent shrugged. "Just wanted to take a walk. How are you two doing?"

"Good," Rebecka said. She took Steopa's hand. The glow from the ring went from dull to a more intense light.

"You should stop by the 'Keller sometime," Vincent said. "They are going to film a movie there."

"Really, that is so cool," Rebecka said. "So what's the movie?"

"Ashes at Dawn."

"Oh my god, that's becoming a movie?" Rebecka curled her lip. "That was the worst twenty dollars I ever spent."

"You've read it?" Vincent asked.

"Yeah, I thought it was going to be a good horror story. Instead I get this vampire-like guy mourning over a woman he killed."

"Apparently it's popular," Vincent said.

"Well, it does have it's selling points. Lots of sex."

Vincent laughed. "You're kidding me."

"I hope you do not mean with the vampire?" Steopa asked.

"That's who gets in the bed most of the time," Rebecka said. "If you were to cut those scenes out, you would have a very short book."

The ring faded to the dull glow.

"What is up with that ring?" Vincent asked.

"Remember Jalmari?"

"Yeah, short vampire, wanted to rip apart the club."
"I found this in his stash."
She held out her hand for Vincent. He ran his finger over the jewel.
"It's warm," he said.
"I noticed," she said. "Yeah, I got a necklace too. But I don't like wearing it."
"It makes you upset," Steopa said.
Rebecka nodded. "Real edgy."
Steopa growled. His eyes were focused on the other side of the park. Vincent turned his head to see. A woman walked through the snow. She headed toward them, but would stop and start to walk away. Then she would turn and continue.
"Oh no," Rebecka said.
"Who is that?" Vincent asked.
"Dorn," Steopa said. He shook his head. His long black pony tail flung over his shoulder.
The woman continued. Her wild white hair flung out from underneath her stocking cap. She pulled the outermost jacket around her body as she got closer.
"Radovitch!" Dorn said. She waved her hands.
"It's Rodovitch," Rebecka said.
Dorn came closer, but Vincent could smell her before he could make out her face.
"Radovitch." Dorn pointed at Vincent. "Who is this?"
"Dorn. Leave," Steopa said.
Dorn's eyes widened. "I know who he is. He's a murderer, an assassin, a foul thing."
"Those are my good points," Vincent said. He flashed her a smile.
Dorn stumbled back into the snow. "Have you seen the new one? The trickster?"
"What?"
Rebecka shook her head. "Ignore her, her mind's gone."
Steopa picked up Dorn. "Leave us, or I will break my promise!"
Dorn tore out of his grip and ran back the way she had came, moving faster than a woman her age should.
Vincent scoffed. "What the hell was that about?"
"She sometimes sees the future," Steopa said.

"You could have killed her."

Steopa shook his head. "That would be a mercy. I will not be merciful to her."

Vincent. Verina voice spoke in his head.

He turned away. *What is it?*

Bored.

How bored?

Very.

Vincent chuckled. "Sorry, I have to go," he said. "Stop by the Rathskeller. John will start bugging me if you don't."

"Perhaps later," Rebecka said.

Vincent waved to them, and then ran out of the park. *You remember the old tannery?*

Yeah.

Meet me there. Vincent headed back to the bookstore.

Verina met him a block away from the event. The line had already stretched to where they were standing.

"Hmm." Vincent walked closer to the crowd. "What do you think?"

"I'd rather be dancing," Verina said.

"Come on, they are filming his book at my club," Vincent said. "Let's see who is behind those books."

Verina shrugged. They walked past the long line. Vincent passed one of the men, who gave him a 'why me?' look. Verina wrapped her long fingers around the door handle and looked up in surprise.

Vincent could feel it now.

Another vampire? Vincent asked.

Feels like it.

They walked in. Vincent bought one of the books titled Hot Ashes. A woman glanced at Vincent and gave him a strange look. He handed the book to Verina. She took his arm. The line snaked through the book shelves. Vincent walked up to a couple of younger women at the front of the line.

"Hey thanks for holding our spot," Vincent said. *Remember, we asked you*, he thought. They smiled and nodded. Vincent and Verina got in line behind them.

Five minutes to midnight. The crowd behind Vincent and Verina surged ahead. A man in a business suit came out of the back of the store. He walked up to a podium and coughed. The crowd became silent.

"I want to thank you all for coming," he said. "I want to introduce you to the man that brought Stephan Ashington back from the dead. Nathan Stout!"

The line surged forward. Verina slammed her pointed heel into the foot of the woman foot who almost knocked her over. The vampire came out of the back of the store. Vincent laughed. Verina rolled her eyes. The rest of the crowd screamed.

Nathan Stout wore a long black leather coat with a tall black top hat. He had pulled the lace down from the brim of his hat to cover his pale face. Vincent admired the red silk shirt and black leather pants that Nathan wore.

That must have set him back a few hundred dollars. Vincent thought.

More. That coat is an antique.

'I think I have the same one in my closet.' Vincent laughed.

Nathan Stout shook a few hands of the people in the front of the store. Under the lace, his face glowed like a half-moon. His black beard was trimmed close to his chin. He took off his hat and the women screamed again. His black braid had a single black ribbon holding it back. Nathan glanced in Vincent and Verina's direction and gave them a small smile.

He sat down and waved to the woman at the front of the line. She squealed and walked up to the table, holding her copy of the book like a religious icon. She took off her jacket after she handed Nathan her copy. She wore a low cut shirt. Nathan signed his name on the cover and then motioned her closer with a curl of his finger. He reached up and signed her breasts.

Verina rolled her eyes again. Nathan caught Vincent's eye and smirked. Then Nathan gave the crowd a wide smile, showing off his fangs.

"He's got style," Vincent said.

Verina gave Vincent a blank look. She flipped the book over in her hand and read the back cover. The line moved ahead. Nathan stood up and had his picture taken with an elderly woman. He stopped the photographer so he could put his hat back on. Then he pulled down the lace and nodded.

Vincent and Verina were next in line. Nathan waved them over, grinning. Vincent held out his hand. Nathan shook it with a firm grip.

"You've never read my books," Nathan said, low enough so the crowd could not hear. His voice had a soft English accent to it. It was not as posh as Ogden's. Nathan's sounded rougher like he was from the working class.

"No, but your movie is being filmed at my club," Vincent said.

Nathan took the book from Verina. He signed it, and gave it back with a wink. They moved on. The girl behind them screamed and almost collapsed.

Verina opened the title page, and read what Nathan had written. "I would like to meet you again. I have not seen many blood suckers around."

Vincent smirked. "Well, I hope he doesn't do anything to piss me off," he said.

Verina laughed. "You were the one who said he had style."

"Yeah, I'm already jealous."

"So what do you want to do now?" Verina asked.

"You want to see the old place?"

"There is nothing else to do. Too bad about the Mackenzie place."

"Their fault for having all that bootlegged bourbon around," Vincent said.

Verina stopped to light a cigarette. "I know, I should have quit these then."

Vincent laughed.

North of the university and just on the outer edges of the old money part of the city sat the area where the new money had first settled. Those families had moved on, or were all laying in Forest Grove. Now the area had become a rough part of town.

The city had opened the door decades ago to landlords to buy up all the old homes. Unfortunately, it was also the time the mayor was enjoying kickbacks, so the grand scheme to bring families back failed. The property owners here were nothing more than slum lords, many times making more money by leaving the houses empty than by fixing them up and letting people live in them.

And Vincent thought it was all good karmic revenge. Most of the old families that lived here had made their money by stepping on the poor, abusing their power, and just being assholes. Joshua had lived here. Vincent had gone by his old home many times. The more it fell into decay, the more Vincent felt vindicated.

There it was. Verina put her cigarette out with her boot. "What a dump."

It was. At one time this place had been an example of Victorian opulence. But now it was sitting in the dark, with broken windows, boarded up doors, and siding falling off. Vincent could hear heartbeats inside. He knew that who ever was in there was not paying for the right to be there.

"I remember the first night I met you," Verina said. "Joshua almost got his throat ripped out then." She studied the building. "It is still there?"

Vincent nodded. "At least it was a few years ago."

"Well, should we go in?"

Vincent stared at the house for a moment. Even with the cover of snow, it could never look peaceful.

"Well?"

CHAPTER 4

Vincent and Verina walked down the small space between the houses and entered the backyard. The once beautiful gardens were now a small yard with a smashed fountain. Verina walked over to the pieces of the fountain and kicked some of the debris aside with her high-heeled boots.

"Joshua would have flipped if he saw this," she said. She bent down and picked up the head of the statue that had been in the middle of the fountain. Someone had spray painted it white and red.

"Serves him right," Vincent said.

Verina tossed Vincent the statue head. "Remember the night I got you free, you chased him out here."

Vincent nodded. "I gutted him over there." He nodded in the direction of an apartment building.

Verina walked over to Vincent. "I will give him this: he didn't beg."

"He should have." Vincent tossed the head over the fence and into the next yard.

"I take it no one lives here," Verina said.

Vincent shook his head. "I can hear heartbeats, but I doubt they are there legally."

Verina smiled. "Should be fun."

The back door hung off its hinges. The plywood that had covered it laid on the floor of the doorway. Vincent walked pass the threshold and did not feel any barrier. Verina stepped in the house, checking the floor before she put her high-heeled boots down. The walls had been ripped apart. Vincent stepped over the remains of a sink in the entry hall. The wood paneling was gone. The massive chandelier had disappeared half a century ago; only the large hook in the ceiling remained.

There were people in the house. The unmistakable scents of drugs, sweat, and urine filled the air. One of the squatters sat in the old foyer. He glanced at Vincent and Verina with jaundiced eyes.

"What the fuck?" He tried to get up, but his body shook and he sat back down.

"Don't mind us," Vincent said.

They walked by him. He stared at them as they passed. Beyond the foyer was a little room, which at one time had been the butler's closet. They passed through the room and went down into the basement.

The stairs swung as they walked down. As they descended, the smell of human waste became stronger. Vincent shut down his nostrils. Verina waved her hand in front of her face and wrinkled her nose.

The wine cellar was gone, the old furnace lay in ruins, and piles of mattresses had been laid on the ground. Two more people were in the basement. One lay on a filthy mattress, his arm flung out behind him. A metal pipe laid discarded on the floor next to his hand. The ashes from the smoked drug fanned out from it. His fingers still clung to the lighter.

A skinny white woman stood up on legs that were too thin. She smiled at Vincent. Her mouth had gaps were teeth had been. She pulled her dirty hair back. Scratches and abscesses covered her skin.

Verina lit a cigarette; she didn't smoke it. She waved it front of her, making the smoke fill the air. Vincent allowed himself to smell again. The smell of tobacco was a lot better than the aroma of human waste. The blond walked up to Vincent.

"You want some?" she asked, offering a pipe to him.

Vincent shook his head.

"Do you have any money?"

Vincent shook his head again. He walked past her, heading toward the old coal box. The blond stopped him.

"I could suck your cock."

Verina covered her mouth with the hand holding the lit cigarette. Her shoulders shook. Vincent turned toward the blond, dropping his glamor at the same time. The blond's eyes and mouth opened wide.

"I think you better leave," he hissed and stomped in her direction.

The blond screamed and shoved her way past Verina. They watched her stumble up the stairs. Verina waved. Vincent turned back around and walked over to the coal box. He paused at the small door.

Verina came over to him. "You could still be here."

He opened the door to the six-by-six room with ornate metal work on the inside. The iron had strange symbols twisted and stamped into it. Vincent ran his fingers over the rusted metal.

"How long was I here?" he asked.

He stepped inside. On the far wall were the scratches he had left. In the walls hung two thick iron hooks. The chains that had held Vincent in this room had hung from those hooks. He fingered one of them.

"How did he do it?" Vincent asked. "How could he have kept me here?"

Verina stood outside the room. "I never understood how, either."

Vincent scoffed. "He never threw anything out, even a guy he killed."

Verina crossed her arms. "Why did you want to come back

here?"
"I don't know," Vincent said. "It was where we first met. You came down here to get a bottle of wine."
"I found you." Verina nodded. "Kept in here like a beast."
"Thank you."
Verina waved her hand. "You always say that."
Vincent smiled. "I always mean it."
She took his arm. "We should go. I need to do some dancing."
They crossed the basement and started to walk up the stairs. Two men appeared at the top of the stairs. One held a piece of pipe; his friend had a large knife.
Verina put her cigarette out. She grinned at Vincent. Vincent yelled up the stairs. "Can I help you gentlemen?"
"You scared Kitcat," the pipe wielder said.
"I don't know how," Vincent said. "I just told her no."
"You're going to apologize," said the one holding the knife.
"No, I don't think so," Vincent said.
"Damn it," Verina said. "Can I just slit their throats?"
"What the hell did she say?" said the knife wielder.
"Sure, what the hell," Vincent said.
Verina sliced through both men's necks with her long fingernails before Vincent had finished nodding. They crumbled to the floor and rolled down the stairs. Vincent stepped aside as the bodies hit the bottom of the steps.
Verina cleaned out her nails. Vincent joined her at the top of the stairs. "Aren't you hungry?"
Verina's upper lip curled. "I would want them to bathe first."
Vincent laughed. They went into the foyer. Kitcat sat on the stairs, holding her head in her hand. She looked up and jumped.
"How's it going?" Vincent asked.
Kitcat screamed and ran up the stairs. Verina giggled. She hooked her arm in Vincent's and they walked out of the house. Verina patted his forearm.
"Do you want to come see the band?" she asked.
Vincent shook his head. "I have had enough fun for the night."
"You're getting old," she said.
"You're older than me."
Verina wiggled her finger in his face. "You are not supposed to bring that up."

"Sorry," Vincent grinned. He pushed her finger away. "I have to get back, anyway. Business things to do."

"Ugh, I feel sorry for you," Verina said.

"It okay, I don't have to hunt."

"I don't either. But I still do, sometimes."

"It's not like it's boring," Vincent said. "I killed a drug dealer last week. Bastard shot me."

Verina paused. "Shot you? You let him shoot you?"

"I didn't see the gun."

She tilted her head to one side. "That's not like you."

"What?"

"The last time I saw you shot was when we were surrounded at that still. And that was at least four gunmen."

"I wasn't paying attention."

"Perhaps. I will see you later." She lit a cigarette and blew the smoke out. As she did, she turned to a mist and disappeared into the night.

Vincent misted and headed back to the Rathskeller. After Lorelei and him went over the contract, Vincent retired. The stupor that took him was strong. He did not hear any noises that he normally did during his sleep, until he heard someone knocking on his door.

Vincent groaned. He pushed open the small door that was the entrance to his bed. He had walled up the sides of a four-poster bed as a room within a room. He rolled out of bed and grabbed a blanket. He wrapped the blanket around his midsection. What was going on that couldn't wait? he thought. He opened the door.

Lorelei tried to hide her smirk. "Sorry," she said. "They're going to start filming and they are doing more night shots. I wanted to warn you."

"That could have waited," Vincent said, starting to close his door.

Lorelei shook her head, she had dyed her hair blue. "Someone is here and asking for you. The author."

"Really? What time is it?" he asked.

"Nearly seven."

"What? When was sunset?"

"About an hour ago." Lorelei grinned. "You overslept."

"Weird. All right, tell him in a few minutes."

Lorelei ran down the hall. Vincent shut the door and dropped the blanket. No reason to dress up tonight. He threw on dark pants, a blue shirt, and tennis shoes.

He went downstairs. The Rathskeller did not look like it had the night before. Along one side of the club, film equipment had been set up. The décor had been changed. The mannequins on the balcony were gone, replaced by fake coffins. The stage had a raised platform placed in the middle of it.

Nathan Stout sat at the bar, talking to Lorelei. Next to Nathan sat the man who had introduced him at the bookstore. Nathan was still dressed in black and silk, but he had toned down his look for tonight as well. Nathan nodded to Vincent as he approached.

"So this is Vincent," Nathan said, not waiting for Lorelei to introduce them. Nathan pointed to his companion. "This is Harry Jones, my agent slash manager slash friend."

Harry stood up and gave Vincent a firm handshake. "This is an interesting place you have here."

You're a flipping Vassal, Vincent thought. "Lorelei takes care of all the details, you should thank her," he said.

Lorelei poured Harry a drink. Nathan had a glass of water in front of him. Vincent walked around to the other side of the bar. "I've never read any of your books," he said.

"Most men do not like them, so don't feel bad," Nathan said. "Eighty percent of my readers are women."

Vincent leaned on the bar. Lorelei tensed as a member of the film crew brought in more large crates and slammed them down.

"Don't worry, these guys are good," Nathan said.

She picked up a rag and wiped down the bar. "Oh, before I forget, Johnny is at his studio. Andi is coming in to help out."

She winked at Vincent. He wasn't hungry, but he would be soon. "Great, what time?" he asked.

"Soon. She had a late class," Lorelei said.

There was a crash from somewhere on the dance floor. Lorelei cringed. She threw down the rag. "I have to check on something."

She went into the back store room. Nathan pushed his water away and smiled. "Nice set-up here. Do you do your hunting here too?"

Vincent glanced at Harry. Nathan waved his hand to dismiss him. "Don't worry about him," he said. "Harry is my good friend, aren't you."

"As long as you are making me money," Harry said.

Nathan laughed.

"If you think that having him as a client is weird, you have never met some of the other people I have worked with," Harry said.

Vincent shook his head. "So what is with the uber goth look?" he asked.

"They expect it," Nathan said. "My first book I did not allow any photos taken of me. A rumor started on the Internet that I was a vampyre, with a y, you know?"

Vincent nodded. He knew. If it wasn't for vampire life-stylers, the Rathskeller would have closed years ago.

"So Harry suggests that I really play it up. Never be seen eating food. React if people have garlic or crosses on them. And of course the outfits," Nathan smiled. "By the fourth book, my fans expected it. Of course, every time some reporter asked me about it. They say, it's just an act, right? And I assure them it's like Ozzy Osbourne. You wouldn't expect him to show up at a concert wearing a tux, would you?"

Andi came into the bar from the back. She was dressed in regular clothes tonight as well. She smiled at Vincent. Vincent made the quick introductions. Nathan kissed the back of Andi's hand.

"You will have to excuse us," Vincent said. He took Andi's hand.

Nathan grinned again. "I see. When they come to you, it is so much easier, isn't it?" he laughed.

Andi gave Vincent an odd look. Vincent opened the half door to the bar. He leaned over to Nathan. "Well, the trick is to get them to come back," he said.

Nathan laughed. Vincent patted him on the shoulder, then left with Andi. They went to the private room he had behind the stage. Lorelei had hung a No Admittance sign on it, so the crew had stacked chairs in front of it. Vincent growled.

He moved the stack of chairs and unlocked the door. Andi went inside. She sat down on the couch. "He really is a vampire," she said. "Damn, how's he do it?"

Vincent shook his head. "I don't know."

"I thought it was a story, you know, like that one about that homeless guy those college girls have sex with."

Vincent laughed. "What?"

"It's the first story you hear when you live at the dorms. There is this homeless guy that lives in Greenwoods and a lot of the women at the college have done the nasty with him."

"He rapes them?"

"No, they can't resist him. I don't know. I used that cross country track all the time, never saw him."

Andi unbuttoned the top of her shirt. She tilted her head. Vincent slid next to her. He ran his fingers over her neck.

"Are you sure you want it from the neck tonight?" he asked.

"I don't care," she said.

Andi didn't flinch when he bit her neck. She patted his head as he fed. Vincent ran his hand up her side, she pushed it down.

"Stop it," she said.

Vincent had his fill. He kissed her neck as he pulled away. Andi sighed. Vincent patted her knee.

"What is it?" he asked.

"I didn't get that extra part. Apparently, they were looking for skanky women."

"Maybe that's a good thing," Vincent said. "You look too classy."

"I guess, but it would have been fun."

She stood up and pulled Vincent off the couch. "Hey! Who is that new guy?"

"New security guy? Chuck. Swen hired him to help out with the movie," Vincent said.

"He's really nice," Andi said. "And he knows what Savate is. I'll have to invite him to one of the competitions."

Vincent touched Andi's mind. She had no idea that Chuck was different. He didn't think it was his place to say anything. Andi was a smart girl, she would figure it out soon enough. Chuck didn't seem dangerous and Vincent would know.

Andi walked out of the room. Vincent stood at the doorway and watched Nathan talking to Harry at the bar. Andi walked pass Nathan. He turned around on his bar stool and said something to her. Andi shook her head. She walked away, rolling her eyes.

A woman from the film crew came up to Nathan with some paperwork. She blushed as she talked to him. When she walked away, she kept looking over her shoulder at him. Vincent shook his head.

Nathan behaved himself. Vincent relaxed. It felt strange having an unfamiliar vampire around that did not want to fight for the nightclub. Vincent went over to the bar. Nathan gave Vincent a wink.

"So you just feed a little, then?" Nathan asked.

"Yeah."

"Miss the hunt?"

"Sometimes, but this is easier," Vincent lied. He did miss the hunt, but it was too easy for him.

Harry stood up. "We have to get going."

"That's right, that interview at the local TV station," Nathan said. "What channel?"

"Twelve," Harry said.

"That's a good number." Nathan laughed. "I will see you around, Vincent. Now I have to get my fangs sharpened."

Harry and Nathan walked towards the door. Nathan stopped Andi and said something to her. Andi nodded. Nathan smiled. Then Harry tapped his shoulder and they left.

Lorelei came out of the back room. "Where's Mr. Stout?"

"He had to leave," Vincent said. "TV interview."

"He's a bit of an arrogant prick, if you ask me."

"I like him."

"You're a lot like him." Lorelei leaned against the bar.

"So I'm a prick?"

"You're a cute prick."

A few hours of watching the tedium that was making a movie, Vincent got bored. He looked at the clock. John would be closing up his shop soon. Vincent went out the back way and up to John's shop. The door was locked, but Teddybear let him in.

The small waiting area was full. Teddybear wiped her shaved head and shrugged. "Busiest night in years," she said.

"I can see that," Vincent said.

"I had to stop an hour ago. I ran out of ink."

"What about your appointments?"

"They got done, but then all these walk-ins." Teddybear smiled. "My hand's cramping, but he money is good."

"John busy?"

"Catch him quick. He's cleaning up."

Vincent walked past Teddybear's booth. Then past Jay's, who

had a woman in his chair. They were looking over some twisted pieces of metal. The shop always had a background smell of blood. Vincent found it comforting. As he approached John's booth, the smell of bleach overpowered the blood smell.

John closed the lid to his autoclave and went over to the sink as Vincent walked into John's booth. He sat down in the chair. John dried off his hands and turned around.

"God, what a night," he said. He nodded towards Jay's booth. "Poor Jay, they just keep coming in."

"What's going on?" Vincent asked.

"It's the movie," John said. "Most of the people outside are hoping to catch a glimpse of the actors. Some come in here to get out of the cold. And a few stay to get inked."

A sharp smell of burnt skin hit Vincent's nostrils. Someone cried out in Jay's booth. John shrugged. "Or get burned," he said.

Vincent chuckled.

"What are you doing up here?" John asked.

"Watching them make a movie is boring," Vincent said.

"You should have heard the screams when that one actor walked by," John said. He opened a soda and took a drink.

"You know, we have had some pretty big names appear downstairs, and I have never seen that sort of reaction before." He shook his head. His dreds bounced around his face.

"I stopped by Nathan's book signing. Same thing," Vincent said.

"I don't understand it. Lorelei liked the books, but she's not like the rest of those women."

Vincent felt Steopa and Rebecka approaching. He smiled. "John, you're going to have visitors."

"Who?"

Vincent heard Teddybear open the shop door. John stood up to see over the side of his booth. His face split into a large grin. "You could have said."

"Surprise."

Rebecka walked into the booth. She hugged her brother, lifting him off the floor. Vincent chuckled. Steopa loomed over the chair. He leaned down.

"I have to speak to you," he said.

"Okay," Vincent said. He got up and left with Steopa. They walked down the block. A few people gave Vincent odd looks. He

rubbed his arms and realized he had forgotten to put on a coat.
"What's up?" he asked.
"Someone dumped a body in front of my door tonight," Steopa said.
"Really?"
"No blood, and missing a few pounds of flesh, too." Steopa's voice never wavered from its low, Slavic accented tone.
"Did you piss anyone off lately?"
"No," Steopa said. "At least none that are still a threat."
"Well, there is another one of us in town."
"You've met him?" Steopa asked.
Vincent nodded. "He's the author of those books."
Steopa cocked his head to one side. "You are pulling my leg."
Vincent shook his head.
"He should dispose of his meals with more discretion," Steopa said.
"It might have been him. But there are human psychos too."
Steopa nodded. "Yes. If that is the case, then we have a cannibal."
Vincent had a mental image of the body, with the missing pounds of flesh. He chuckled. "Well, you can't blame them for being hungry."
Steopa brushed some snow off his shoulders. "If it is the other vampire..." His green eyes flashed.
"I'll tell you anything I find out."
"Good."
John and Rebecka walked down the street. Rebecka glanced in their direction.
Steopa told you? Rebecka asked Vincent, while she still talked to John.
Did you see the body? Vincent asked.
I almost stepped in it.
Vincent grinned. He reached up and patted Steopa on the shoulder. "You two want to do anything?"
Steopa shook his head. "No, Rebecka and I have plans."
Steopa took Rebecka's hand and wrapped his arm around her. He kissed her on her cheek. Vincent glanced at John. He hadn't noticed; he was zippering up his leather jacket.
Vincent coughed. "So, you know that vampires can't reproduce

that way."

Rebecka slugged Vincent in the shoulder.

"I'm just saying!"

Rebecka bent down and picked up a snowball and she threw it. It hit him in the midsection. Vincent grabbed a snowball and threw it at Rebecka. She dodged it and threw another at Vincent. It hit John.

"Sorry!" Rebecka said, while making another snowball.

Steopa took a few steps back. Vincent threw another one at Rebecka. She dove and it hit Steopa. Everyone paused. Steopa walked over to Vincent. He grabbed Vincent's collar. Then he bent down and picked up a pile of snow. He slammed it down on Vincent's head.

John laughed. He leaned up against the building, his body shaking with the laughs. Steopa released Vincent's collar. His lips curled back at the corners. He smiled.

The smile on his face startled Vincent. He had never seen Steopa smile. Rebecka giggled.

"We have to go. Bye." Rebecka hugged John.

The snow swirled up around them and they were gone. John covered his mouth with his arm and giggled. "You did ask for it, you know," John said, pushing his glasses up on his nose.

"Yeah, I did."

John left Vincent. He could hear John giggling all the way back to the shop. He shook the rest of the snow out of his hair. Why hadn't I told Steopa about Verina? he thought. She is new in town, too. She would not be that messy of an eater, at least she had not been.

CHAPTER 5

The next night, Vincent started to walk down the stairs, then stopped. He wasn't hungry. He had no reason stay at the club while they were filming. He walked out the back door and past the trailers that had been set up along the alleyway.

Verina, he thought.

What's up?

Can you believe I am bored?

So am I.

Where are you?

A practice studio.

She told him the address. It didn't take him long to find the place. Verina sat on a couch, her legs crossed, reading a magazine. The bassist and guitarist tuned their instruments. The drummer hammered out beats inside the booth.

Toby gave Vincent a little nod as he entered. He smiled, exposing his fangs for good measure.

"Sorry about the other night," Toby said.

Vincent shrugged. "It's not an issue."

Verina put the magazine down. "I can't believe you are bored."

"It happens." Vincent sat on a chair next to Verina. "That movie is taking forever."

He rubbed his hands over his face.

Verina nodded. "I know. I was at the last video Toby and the guys shot."

He turned to Toby. "Do you mind if I kidnap Verina for awhile?"

Toby nodded, but then turned to the bassist. "What riff was that?"

"Where are we going?" Verina asked.

"Come on," Vincent said.

"Where are we going?"

"I want to show you something interesting."

Verina pointed a long fingernail at him. "I will not go into an old house."

"It's not an old house."

Verina pulled her fur boots over to her and put them on. Toby glanced in their direction, then turned to yell at the bassist again. Verina stopped Vincent at the door.

"Where are we going?" Her tone matched a nanny scolding a child.

"Forest Grove."

Verina glanced back at the band. The drummer and the guitarist watched Toby and the bassist arguing over a riff the bassist wanted to put in the song.

"I suppose it will be quieter," she said.

Outside, Verina waved down a cab. The driver would sneak glances of Verina over his shoulder. She curled her hair around her fingers.

"Why are we going to a cemetery?" she asked.

Verina unzipped her coat to her chest. The driver's eyes went wide. She glared at the driver. He took his eyes off her.

“You remember Forest Grove,” Vincent said.

“Yes,” Verina giggled. “I remember you running from those gangsters.”

“Bullets hurt.”

The driver pulled up to the cemetery. Vincent paid the man, then leaned over.

“What do you think of her?” he asked.

“You are a lucky man,” the driver said.

“I was.”

Vincent's voice changed. “Forget who we were.”

The driver's eyes clouded. He put the car in gear and drove off. Vincent grinned. Verina lit a cigarette. She shook her head. “One of these days you are going to run into someone who won't listen to you.”

“Already have.”

“Who?”

“Rebecka. Before she became a vampire, she could block me from messing with her mind.”

Verina cocked her head. “When she was human?”

Vincent nodded.

“I have never heard of a human doing that.”

Vincent shrugged. “She could.”

They walked deeper into the cemetery on top of the snow. Neither of them left any footprints in the light powder. Verina put her cigarette out on a gravestone.

“I think I know where we are going,” she said.

Vincent chuckled.

Dysart Memorial loomed ahead of them in a small valley. The mini-cathedral wasn't the largest tomb in the cemetery. It wasn't even the most impressive, but it did have an interesting past. But only a few knew about it.

Verina smiled. “I remember this place.”

“You're gonna like it even more.” Vincent felt Rebecka and Steopa were there. “You remember I told you about my donor's sister? She's inside.”

Verina moved the angel statue. Vincent jumped down into the old smuggler tunnel. He went ahead as he got to the door to the lowest level. Vincent heard a soft moan. He glanced over his shoulder. Verina smirked.

Rebecka is the one that is linked, right? Verina asked.

Yeah.

Verina covered her mouth, to stifle her laugh. Vincent opened the door a little. Rebecka and Steopa were kissing. Verina placed her long fingers on Vincent's back and looked over his shoulder.

"What a lucky couple," Verina whispered.

Rebecka broke off the kissing. "Vincent."

Vincent waited a moment, then opened the door. Rebecka tucked in her shirt. If vampires could blush, she would have been beet red.

"Hey Rebecka and Steopa, this is my old friend Verina," Vincent said.

Verina stopped and stared at Steopa. Vincent guided her over to a chair. *What is it?* he asked.

Nothing. Just rumors.

"So have you two been busy?" Vincent asked.

Rebecka glared at him.

"Why are you here?" Steopa asked.

"I wanted to show Verina the old place," Vincent said. "She used to frequent here."

Vincent had to look away, Steopa had a stare on him that would drill through walls.

"Why?" Rebecka asked.

"I ran booze," Verina said.

"You were a bootlegger?" Rebecka asked. "That's so cool."

Verina shrugged. "I needed something to do at night."

"Is this the vampire you were telling me about?" Steopa asked.

Vincent shook his head. "No, that one is Nathan Stout."

"Steopa mentioned something last night, but I wasn't sure if that's who you meant," Rebecka said.

"Yeah, he likes to charm his fans," Verina said. "You should have seen him at the book signing. Toby has groupies with more self control."

Steopa made a noise between a grunt and a sigh. "What does he do with them when he is done?"

Vincent shook his head. "Who knows. Although he kept asking me about hunting." Vincent paused. "A bit annoying actually."

Verina stared at Steopa. When he moved his gaze from Vincent to her. She studied her long fingernails. "Can we go to the top floor?"

“I would like too, but the upper level is off limits now,” Vincent said.

“Why?”

“We made a promise. To keep it safe,” Steopa said.

Verina adjusted her fur lined coat. She flicked off some snow. “What is up there?”

“I can't tell you,” Vincent said.

Verina shrugged. “Whatever.”

After a moment of strained silence, Rebecka pointed to the book case. The ring on her hand glowed. “We are thinking of bringing in some more pieces of furniture.”

Verina stood up and walked over to Rebecka. She took Rebecka's hand. Pulling her hand up so Verina could look at the ring. “Where did you get that?”

Rebecka pulled her hand back. “I found it.”

Verina looked surprised. “I have not seen that in centuries.”

She started to dig through her handbag. Throwing some of the contents on the floor.

“Spit it out,” Vincent said.

Verina closed her handbag, then bit her fingernail. She glanced at Rebecka. “The last vampire I saw wear that was attacked by a small group of Crusaders. They were massacred,” she said. “That ring is powerful.”

“What are you talking about?” Rebecka asked.

“He just pointed and they cooked in their skins.”

“It does get warm,” Rebecka said, moving the ring around her finger.

“Maybe it's a dud now,” Vincent said.

“Or the necklace has to be worn too,” Steopa said.

“I'm not wearing that necklace,” Rebecka said. “It makes me bitchy.”

“You found the necklace too? What about the bracelet?” Verina asked. “Does the blood still flow inside it?”

Rebecka nodded. “The bracelet is gone.”

“It was destroyed in a fight,” Steopa said. He put his arm around Rebecka and pulled her closer.

Verina sat down beside Rebecka. “That ring can burn up a mob. We were trapped. The knights did not know what we were; they only wanted to hunt down the pagans. My friend was wearing that ring. The knights surrounded us, and he waved his hand. All the knights started to burn. It saved our lives that night."

"When was this?" Steopa asked.

"During the Northern Crusades," Verina said.

"Where did he get the ring?" Rebecka asked.

"I don't know," Verina said. "When I saw him years later he wasn't wearing it, but he would not talk to me about it."

"Interesting story," Steopa said.

"I am sure that is the ring," Verina said.

"Why did you come here tonight?" Steopa asked.

Vincent rubbed his goatee. "I invited her," he said.

"This is supposed to be a secret," Steopa said.

"She's the one who showed me this place," Vincent said. "We should thank her."

"What have you been doing with your meals?" Steopa asked. "I hope you are covering your traces."

Verina raised a corner of her mouth, like a snarl. "I am not a messy eater."

"Can you prove it?" Steopa asked.

Vincent stood up. "Verina, maybe we should see how your boyfriend's band is coming along."

"Toby is not my boyfriend."

"Okay, your meal, then," Vincent said, grinning.

"You can be an ass," Verina said.

"That's for sure," Rebecka said.

Verina chuckled. She turned to Rebecka. "If that ring gets really hot, be careful."

Rebecka wrung her hands together, holding them close to her chest. Steopa pulled her closer and kissed her forehead. Verina turned to leave, then stopped.

"We should meet again," she said.

Vincent opened the door to the tunnel. "I'll catch up with you two later."

They did not go back to the recording studio. Instead, they walked by another one of their old hangouts. In its glory years it had been the grandest hotel in Deerbow. Now it had been changed over to single bedroom apartments. Parts of its former glory could be seen on the outside.

Verina paused to reapply her lipstick. "You're jealous aren't you?"

"What do you mean?" Vincent asked.

"Rebecka and Steopa. You looked a little upset when we walked in on them."

"I was surprised," Vincent said. "I didn't expect them to be making out like teenagers."

Verina gave him a doubtful look, then took his arm. "They are lucky. You should be happy for them. The linking rarely happens and most of the time they end up killing each other."

"How many have you seen?" Vincent asked.

"Two. Neither of those couples were as happy as those two are."

Vincent sighed. He held on to Verina's arm. "But you know how I operate, tempt them into my little room. It's been a long time, you know."

Verina laughed. "What brought this on? We play. We pretend. Just to get the humans to let down their guard. It's never real."

"So it's an act with Toby?"

Verina shook her head. "No, he knows. He has those girls for sex. He would never expect me to."

Vincent paused on the other side of the street from the old hotel. "Rebecka is a lot happier now," he said.

"She's happier as a vampire?"

"Well, sometime you have to die to live," he said. "And don't I know it."

Verina smiled. "Yes, you do. Now what do you know about the large Russian?" Verina asked.

"Steopa?"

Verina nodded.

"Lithuanian, originally, I think," Vincent said. "I know he saw some action in World War Two."

"Anything else?" Verina asked.

Vincent shrugged. "Not really."

"Hmm." Verina looked up at the stars for a moment. "I have heard rumors about a giant from Russia. He is famous among some of the European vampires."

"Why?"

"He killed the vampire that attacked him, while she was feeding on him."

Vincent stopped. "Possible, but he must have been very strong before he turned."

"How many humans could fight you?" Verina asked.

"Swen, but he really doesn't count. But Steopa... I know Rebecka said he got hit by a car, and the front end crumbled."

Verina grinned. "If that is the case, then there are more rumors about him."

"Well, I'm sure I will find out about them soon enough."

Verina nodded. "We should head back."

"So how come you heard rumors about Steopa and not Nathan?" Vincent asked.

"His books don't sell well in Europe, for one," she said. "I read a review in Milan that called them crap."

"But you have heard of him?"

"Yes, but only when Toby's band got the job." Verina brushed her hair back with her fingers. "But I would have never thought he was the real deal."

After leaving Verina with Toby, who was in a sulking match with the bassist, Vincent returned to the Rathskeller. He walked past the security guard. The movie crew still had most of the Rathskeller in disarray. Swen and Chuck sat in the bouncer cage, playing cards.

Vincent went inside the cage. The door to the dance floor was open. The security monitors were turned off.

"What happened to the monitors?" he asked.

"Miss Bitch told me to turn them off; some sort of privacy clause," Swen said. He dealt another hand out. "Andi got a part."

"She did?" Vincent smiled.

"Yeah, Mr. Stout asked the director. She's playing a waitress," Swen said.

Chuck nodded. He played with a new lip ring on his face, around it the skin was swollen and red. "She's pretty excited about it," he said.

"At least she won't have to act," Vincent said.

"So have you ever seen her compete?" Chuck asked. "We are going to a competition in a few weeks."

Swen nodded. "A few times. Don't let her small size fool you, she can take down people a few feet taller than herself."

"Is Nathan around?" Vincent asked.

Swen shook his head. "He came in, got her a part, and left."

Chuck pointed to a pile of books. "Signed them all for my sister. I didn't have the heart to tell him that she thinks they are great comedies."

"Cassie loves them," Swen said. "She read me a few passages. They're okay."

Someone announced the filming was starting up again. Vincent leaned against the open doorway and watched the action.

An actress stood behind one of the actors. He had his arm out, holding the actress behind him.

"Stephan, please don't," she said.

Another actor approached them. "What are you doing with Angelica?"

The director yelled, "Cut! Good. Try it again with more fear."

Andi stopped. She glanced over to the door and rolled her eyes when she saw Vincent. He knew she was cold. The latex maid outfit she was wearing made that fact obvious.

The director called action. Andi moved around the background serving drinks. A few more takes, then the director called a break so they could move the cameras.

Andi ran over to the cage. "Give me a flipping coat."

Chuck took off his and handed it to her. Andi put it on and jumped up and down. "Why this outfit?" she asked. "I am freezing my buns off."

"They had us shut our heating down because the blower makes too much noise," Swen said.

Andi leaned up against Chuck. "It was really nice of Mr. Stout to ask for me to be an extra. He's invited Chuck and me to his hotel tomorrow night."

"Are you sure you want to go, Andi?" Vincent asked.

"It's just a little get-together with some of his fans. I'm bringing two of my roommates along, too."

"But you do know-"

Andi rolled her eyes. "Chuck's coming. Besides, I know how to handle myself."

Vincent glanced at Swen. He shrugged. Andi stared at Vincent, making a face, daring him to say no. He nodded. She smiled.

Someone called the crew back. Andi sighed and gave Chuck his coat. She ran out to the floor. Chuck folded his coat over his arm.

"Hey, Vince, don't worry about it," Chuck said. "I'll be there. I can smell trouble."

Swen glanced at Vincent. "Yeah, tell us about that nose of yours."

Chuck shook his head. "I really can't. I promised my dad."

Vincent grinned. "Can we guess?"

Chuck laughed. "Let's just say I do not mind working with a vampire and whatever you are." Chuck pointed to Swen.

One of the crew members came over and shushed them. Swen shut the door with his foot.

"Problem solved," Swen said. "You know, next time that chick comes by and shushes me, I may have to get nasty."

Vincent patted Swen on the shoulder. "Now, now, mellow out." He tuned to Chuck. "You know what Nathan is?"

Chuck nodded. "Yeah, I could smell him before I saw him."

"And if he tries anything?"

Chuck smiled. His teeth had elongated. The grin looked familiar, nothing like a vampire smile. "Don't worry, I can take out a vampire."

CHAPTER 6

I need to replace that, Vincent thought. He had been waking up to the same fabric for over twenty years. He studied the worn cloth at the top of his canopy bed. The blood stain was still noticeable.

He rubbed his beard, sat up and stretched. He opened the small door that served as the entrance to his bed. He slid out and stood up.

He kicked his clothing from the night before over to a corner of his room, across his bare apartment. He had a couch and a few chairs just in case he ever had visitors, but that never happened. Every window was boarded up. There were the days that he could not sleep, no matter how strong the stupor was.

Vincent got dressed. He heard voices from downstairs in the club and groaned. They were still filming the movie. He would have to feed off of John or Lorelei tonight. He sighed as he pulled on his shoes. *I should go on the hunt*, he thought.

"No hunting," he said.

He leaned against his threadbare couch. *When were they gonna finish?* he thought. *If I go hunting...* He shook his head as he left his apartment. He walked down the hall to John and Lorelei's.

Vincent knocked.

"Vince? Open!" The door muffled John's voice.

Vincent let himself in. The mixed smells of curry, garlic, lemon, wine, and cheese hit Vincent like a wall. He covered his nose, then shut down his sense of smell. John came out of the kitchen. He motioned Vincent over to his worktable.

"Sorry about that," he said. "I just wanted to try something different tonight."

"I feel like hunting," Vincent said.

"You haven't done that in, what? Ten years," John said.

"I know."

"What would happen if you did?"

Vincent ran his hands down his legs and shrugged. "I don't think anything weird would. I just don't want to do it."

Water boiled over in the kitchen. John hurried back. "You stopped when Lorelei and I started to help you out, right?" John asked.

Vincent nodded.

"Look, if you think that hunting would be creepy for us, don't," John said. "We have been around you too long."

He felt Rebecka and Steopa approaching. Good, he needed some distraction. "Rebecka's coming," he said.

John leaned out of the kitchen. "Are you sure?"

The glass on the patio door rattled as someone knocked on it.

Vincent grinned. "Very sure."

John hurried to the patio. He slid open the door. Rebecka came inside, brushing the snow off her coat. Steopa removed his fur hat so he could duck to enter. Rebecka sniffed.

She curled her lip back. "What are you cooking?"

"Sorry guys," John said. "I didn't know all of you were gonna stop by."

Steopa placed his hat on the table. “Another one.”
Rebecka sat down. “Yeah, I think they are dumping them there, because they think they won't be found. I don't think they know we are there.”
“Another dead body?” Vincent asked.
Rebecka nodded. Steopa opened his long officer coat. “Yes, this one had been dead far longer though.”
John wiped his hands as he came over to the table. “Dead bodies? Plural?”
“Yeah, two so far,” Rebecka said. She picked up a circuit board from the work table. “No one has seen anything.”
“How do you know?” Vincent asked.
“I have my ways,” Steopa said.
“Anyway,” Rebecka said. “I thought it would be a good idea to see Swen. I want to talk to his friend Grady.”
“The cop?” John asked.
“I can't go and file a report.”
Lorelei, bleary-eyed, came out of the bedroom. She waved to everyone then stumbled over to the table. John went back into the kitchen. He opened the pot. The steam drifted over the table, bringing the smell with it. Steopa grabbed his hat off the table and then held it to his face.
“Can we go downstairs?” Rebecka asked.
“Still filming the movie,” Vincent said.
“Sorry, John,” Rebecka said. “I have to leave.”
“I didn't put that much garlic in it,” John said.
“It's the garlic, and the curry, and the cardamom, and the...” Rebecka sniffed. “Anchovies?”
She ran for the door. Steopa and Vincent joined her in the hallway.
“When I was human that dish would have grossed me out,” she said.
Vincent clenched his fists. “God.”
“What is it?” Rebecka asked.
“I don't need to feed, but I want to hunt,” he said. “I have not had this urge in a long time.”
“What stops you from hunting?” Steopa asked.
“It's too easy,” Vincent said.
Steopa raised his eyebrow. “Easy?”

Vincent played with his beard. “You have never seen me at my best. I always hold back.”

“Why?” Steopa asked.

“Because there was a time I could walk into a house and walk out again in a few minutes. Everyone would be dead. And no one would have a mark on them.”

“How did you do that?” Rebecka asked.

“I can get inside people. All I have to do is put an idea in someone's head and they would come to me.”

“Like you do with the women?” Rebecka asked.

“Similar. I never just pick any woman; she has to be interested in me first.”

Steopa leaned over and asked Rebecka something. She responded. All Vincent caught was, “...rearrange memories.”

Vincent laughed. “I can move memories, capillaries, nerves, you got it.”

Steopa patted Vincent on the back. “You want a challenge.”

Vincent nodded.

“I might be able to help you,” Steopa said. “If you know where to hunt in this town. Come with us tonight. If nothing else we can leave this stinking hallway.”

“Why the hell not,” Vincent said. His voice sounded tired.

They left the back way. Vincent opened the door to the alley. Chuck slammed into him. Chuck grabbed Vincent and tried to get his breath back.

“What is it?” Vincent asked.

“Did Andi come back here?” Chuck asked.

Vincent searched the minds in the club. Andi was not there. He shook his head.

“We went to Mr. Stout's little party. I went to the bathroom, came back and they were talking. A little while later, his friend tells me I have to move my car, I come back. They tell me Andi left.” Chuck lowered his head, breathing hard.

Vincent turned to Rebecka. “Do you still have that cell phone?”

Rebecka nodded and gave it to Vincent. He dialed Andi.

“Won't work,” Chuck said. “Andi hasn't been answering.”

Andi's phone rang. Vincent turned around while he waited for her to answer. Steopa studied Chuck with his brow furrowed.

“Hello,” Andi said.

Odd, Vincent thought, she usually says hey.

"Hey Andi," Vincent said. "Didn't you go to that get-together at Nathan Stout's?"

"No," she said. "Chuck was supposed to pick me up."

"We could use you at the club tonight." Vincent lied.

"I'll be right there," Andi said.

Vincent placed the phone in Rebecka's hand. "Well, she thinks you didn't pick her up."

"What?" Chuck said. His voice echoed through the alley. "I had to put up with him sliming all over the place."

"Chuck, what is happening?" Steopa asked.

Chuck focused on Steopa. "Oh my God, Steopa. I don't really know."

"You know each other?" Vincent asked.

"Yes," Steopa said. "I am a friend of the Navarros."

Chuck turned back to Vincent. "Something didn't smell right there. It made me edgy. Besides, he didn't like me."

"Tell you what, when Andi gets here, go and talk to her. See what's up," Vincent said.

Chuck nodded. "If she'll speak to me."

Two women walking down the street caught Vincent's eye. He watched them go by. He could almost see their veins. They were thin lines glowing along their bodies. A growl formed in the back of his throat. He pulled his attention back to Chuck.

"I'm sure it was just a misunderstanding," Vincent lied.

"Okay."

"Tell you what you do. Tell her we need the booze inventoried. When she comes in, take her to the back, then ask her what happened."

Chuck nodded.

The girls were across the street now. They had paused in front of one of the boutiques. He could just smell their blood. Vincent took a step in their direction. Steopa placed his hand on Vincent's shoulder.

"Vincent," Steopa said.

Vincent rubbed his forehead. What had come over him tonight? He didn't need to go hunting, but his whole body wanted to.

Rebecka smiled at Chuck. "We'll go talk to Lorelei. Explain what you are doing. Come on."

Chuck left with Rebecka. Steopa waited until they had walked back into the building.

"You need to hunt," he said.

Vincent shook his head.

"Why not?" Steopa asked. "We are vampires. We hunt humans."

"I told you why not."

"Because you need a challenge?" Steopa waved his hand. "Bah. You should follow your instinct."

"Follow my instinct! You have no idea what my instinct is."

Steopa spoke low, with no expression on his face. "You hear the heartbeat. And you want to make it beat faster, because it means the blood is pumping. You want to make your prey run. But it is better if you slowly chase them over days and months. The blood is sweeter." Steopa raised his eyebrow.

Vincent nodded.

"Then we will hunt," Steopa said.

"All right. Any place special?"

"I may have a place."

'*Swen came in. He called Grady. I need to talk to him.*' Rebecka spoke in Vincent's mind.

"Rebecka has to stay," Vincent said.

"We could go now."

"Sure."

Steopa jumped up to a fire escape, then to another. He made his way up to the roof. Vincent followed.

"We will go to Woodlawn," Steopa said.

"Woodlawn?" Vincent asked. "This time of night? Sounds like a blast. Do you have permission to go there?

"No vampire has claimed Woodlawn." Steopa folded his fur hat and slid it into an inside pocket. "The humans there hunt each other. They would not notice us."

Woodlawn had its own shroud. Vincent missed looking for the shrouds. Shrouds surrounded people who wanted to die. It was a "kill me" sign to a vampire.

People didn't move to Woodlawn because it was a good place to live. They either were born here, or got stuck here out of bad choices in their life. No one came here on purpose. And the ones that got lost and ended up here tried to leave as fast as possible.

Steopa landed in an empty lot. Filthy snow covered the ground.

Vincent kicked some of the snow aside. Underneath the gray layer were old cans and potato chip bags.

The street had a lot of people, considering the cold temperature. It wouldn't matter how cold it was, these people did not have anywhere else to go. Vincent could taste the amount of drugs that were in the air. Shadows filled the streets. Perfect hunting grounds. Steopa faded into the shadows. Vincent misted.

In his mist form, he was aware. Being a mist only allowed him to move around undetected. He could feel out in front of him. Sensing the ground and potential prey like a snake. He swirled and moved around the ground. He sensed he passed Steopa.

Steopa had his arms crossed, looking down a side street. His eyes glowed. Vincent flowed down the street. Two vehicles were parked in a parking lot. One was an extended cab truck. The other a large work van with no back windows. Vincent read the bumper stickers. He knew what type of person he was dealing with.

He went back to Steopa and solidified. “Skinheads.”

The corners of Steopa's mouth turned up. “I see.”

“So do you think they are here for the bake sale?”

Steopa's grin widened. He faded back into the shadows and walked down the side street. Vincent did the same.

The skinheads were out of their vehicles. All of them carried implements of pain: baseball bats, chains, knives, and a few guns. The skinheads gathered together around one that had the “SS” symbol tattooed on his cheek. He pointed to the small church across the street.

Vincent misted again, and flowed over the snow to the front of the church. It sat in a rented store front. The cardboard signs in the window welcomed anyone, including gays. Vincent felt the minds of the skinheads. They were easy to read. All of them shared the same thought.

The group crossed the street. Vincent solidified and stepped out of the shadows. He smiled one of his best disarming smiles. “Ah, Gentlemen, out for a little trouble, are we?”

The leader paused, and the group as a whole stopped. All of them changed their hand holds on their weapons, each taking on a threatening pose. Vincent maintained his smile. He had surprised them, but the pause would not last long.

Get out-of-da-way, faggot!” The leader shouted.

Vincent giggled. "Oh dear, assume I'm gay, because of my hair, or was it the fact I can put two syllables together?"

One of the larger skinheads rushed forward. As he raised his baseball bat to swing at Vincent, Vincent caught the bat with his hand and threw the man over the group. He hit the truck behind them, denting the hood. Vincent's smiled never wavered.

"You will have to do better than that," Vincent said.

They rushed him. Vincent misted. The ones in the front tried to stop. The ones in the back did not stop at the same time. The crowd surged and tumbled over each other.

Vincent picked out one of the men in the back of the group. When the man breathed in, Vincent slid inside. He took over the man's body. A twitch of the nerves here and a pull on the tendons there. He took his hijacked body and raised the knife it held. He stabbed the man in front of him. Then he escaped through the exhaled breath. The man who had been stabbed turned around and slammed his bat against the now free man's body.

A brawl started out among the closest skinheads. Vincent moved to the other side of the mob. He solidified and grabbed one at random. Vincent snapped his neck back and buried his fangs into the man's skin. The part of the group that saw Vincent turned and ran back to their vehicles.

The first one reached the van. The van moved forward. It skidded at an angle and then tumbled. It rolled over the unlucky ones who could not move out of the way. When the van came to a crashing halt, Steopa stood behind it. He lifted his head. His eyes burned red.

Vincent threw the drained body down. "Come on!"

The small group gathered together. They still held their weapons out, but their hands shook. Vincent growled.

Someone in the group fired a gun.

The bullet ripped through Vincent. He looked down at the hole in his chest and grinned. Two more shots. These missed Vincent, because he had turned to mist, sliding around the neck of the shooter.

Steopa strode across the street. He roared like a large feline. The small group bolted. Steopa grabbed two of them and slammed them together, knocking them out. Vincent solidified around the man's neck, his arm inside the man's body.

"Try to breathe, asshole," Vincent said in his ear.

The man gasped and tried to pull Vincent's arm out of his throat. Vincent yanked his arm out and tore open the skinhead's throat.

Vincent looked around. Steopa had just taken the head off another one. He threw the corpse against the van. The only one left was the leader. Vincent turned to him. "So, what do you want to do?"

The leader backed up into the wall of the church. Vincent walked over to the man. He placed his hands on the man's shoulder like they were old friends. The leader shuddered under his touch. Steopa kicked one of the corpses aside as he approached.

"He asked you a question," Steopa said.

"I, I, I," the leader squirmed under Vincent's touch.

Steopa lunged forward. The leader slipped out of Vincent's grip and ran down the street. Vincent chuckled. Steopa motioned with his hand toward the running man, and bowed. Vincent took off.

Vincent caught the man before he reached the intersection. He got his hand around the leader's heart as the man stopped running. Vincent squeezed and released the heart. The pressure was enough to make the heart pause for a moment, but not to stop it. Vincent wanted to play.

The leader stumbled forward a few steps. Before his face hit the snow, Vincent picked him up and stood him up. He placed his fingernail against the man's neck and slid it across. The blood welled up in the cut, then flowed down the man's chest. He pulled the man into the shadows and drank as much blood as he could before the man's heart stopped. Vincent giggled and let him fall on to the dirty snow.

Vincent returned to Steopa, laughing. "Man, that was fun."

Steopa picked up one of the guns. He walked over to a corpse. He bent down, removed the man's wallet, then fired one shot into the man's head. He repeated it with every corpse. When he had finished he tossed the gun over to the van.

Vincent admired his work. "Looks good. Gang warfare?"

Steopa nodded. "Possible. The headless one will be hard to explain." He handed Vincent a few of the wallets.

Vincent chuckled. "Spoils."

They went to the nearest roof. They removed the money and threw the wallets over the side of the building. Vincent slapped the bills in his one hand. "It's been ages since I did that. The biggest payout was this bootlegger. He had about a half a million in his truck."

Steopa buttoned up his coat. "Rebecka did not like to take the money at first. She felt it was stealing."

"Sounds like Rebecka."

"Now, she takes the money and the valuables." Steopa shrugged. "I never bothered with the trifles."

Sirens came to a stop close by. Steopa jumped to the next building, followed by Vincent. They left the area, taking the rooftops when they could. When they had to take the ground, they stayed in the darker areas of the streets.

On the roof of the Rathskeller, Vincent turned to Steopa. "I have heard a rumor that you killed the vampire that was feeding on you."

Steopa looked over the city, his expression wooden. "Did Rebecka tell you?"

Vincent shook his head. "Verina did. She's not sure it was you."

Steopa leaned against the ventilation shaft. "It is true," he said. "I was lucky."

"How'd you do it?" Vincent asked.

"I was able to get my firearm between her and I," Steopa said. "I pulled the trigger. She let go of me. I made a stake from a nearby branch and pinned her to the ground."

"Wow," Vincent said. He reached in his back pocket and pulled out the wad of cash. "I should buy you a drink."

Steopa chuckled. Then he looked out over the cityscape. "I want to thank you."

"For what?" Vincent asked.

"Rebecka. You helped her out when she started to change. She could have been so frightened that she would never have had the will to come find me."

"I dunno about that," Vincent said. "She was strong. It was just... she'd rather live in her own head, you know."

Steopa nodded.

"So, you two are very close."

Steopa turned around. "Your meaning?"

"The other night, you two were locking lips." Vincent waited for Steopa to say something. Steopa remained quiet. "How? I mean, why?"

Steopa walked over to Vincent and leaned against the cinder block. "I am not sure, but she has become my love. Physical intimacy should be impossible for our kind. Yet, since Rebecka and I became linked, we are intimate."

"How intimate?"

"We have not had sex. I still think we are physically incapable." Steopa rubbed his chin. "Yet that does not explain the Dhamphirs. Or my daughter."

Vincent stopped himself from staring at Steopa. "You have a daughter?"

Steopa nodded. "She was conceived the night I became a vampire. Before I fully changed, you understand. She lives in Vladivostok now."

"She's a vampire, too?" Vincent asked. "But you were... Oh, I see, you did not become a vampire right away."

"Correct, I did not change until after..." He waved his hand. "Perhaps it only can happen every other century."

Vincent looked over the side of the building. Lights were on inside John and Lorelei's apartment. "And maybe some of us just never will," he said. "I'm sure Rebecka is worried about you."

Steopa shook his head. "No, she is not."

Vincent tilted his head. Steopa did not seem upset.

"You know?"

Steopa tapped the side of his head. "She is waiting for us."

Vincent jumped to the patio. Rebecka opened the door. She glanced over her shoulder and sighed.

Andi sat on the couch, blowing her nose. Dried tears lined her cheeks. She wiped her red eyes. Rebecka returned to the small dining table with Swen. Swen's cell phone sat on the table in front of him. Vincent could hear John talking to Chuck in the kitchen. Lorelei poured a glass of wine at the small bar.

"Welcome to the nut house," she said.

Steopa took a seat next to Rebecka. Lorelei motioned Vincent closer. "Andi is all messed up. She's insisting that they never went to that writer's tonight, yet Chuck's got pictures. Can you talk to her?"

Vincent sat down next to Andi. She looked at him over her tissue, her eyeliner smearing down her face. "You gonna think I'm mad too?"

He shook his head. "No." He laid his arm around her shoulders and touched the base of her skull with his fingers.

He started to probe her mind. Everything seemed normal, until he hit a wall. He could not get around whatever it was. Vincent tried to sneak in through the sense memory. The wall was there. He tried to move around to the instincts, nothing. Just a damn mental wall.

"Andi, do you have a headache?" Vincent asked.

"I did earlier." Andi sagged, like she wanted to melt into the couch. She sobbed. "Why doesn't anyone believe me?"

Vincent glanced over to Lorelei. She sighed and came over to Andi. "Come on, we'll go talk."

Andi went with Lorelei. Vincent stood up. A block. Not just rearranging memories, but a block. He cursed.

In the kitchen, Vincent tapped Chuck on the shoulder. "You only left her alone with Nathan once, correct?"

Chuck shook his head. "Twice."

He took a sip of the beer in his hand. A small pile of empty bottles filled the sink. A quick math equation in Vincent's head made it out to three per person. That was if Lorelei developed a taste for beer and Swen started to drink domestic.

"When you came back, was she acting funny?" Vincent asked.

Chuck thought. "No, but her eyes looked different for a moment." He took another sip. "I could smell that damn vampire on her too. He made it clear he did not like me."

Chuck finished the beer. "Fucking jerk. He knows my ears are good. I heard that flea spray comment. He doesn't like werewolves, big fucking deal."

Vincent glanced at John. John did not look surprised. In fact he looked like he had heard it too many times that night. Chuck growled. John moved away from him. Vincent put his arm around Chuck and dragged him out of the apartment and into the hallway.

Chuck slumped against the wall. Vincent shook Chuck.

"Andi has a block on her memories. She will not remember shit, okay," Vincent said. "I could try to unblock it, but I might fry her brain. What I want you to do is play stupid boyfriend. Pretend that she is right this time. The more you try to convince her what happened, happened. The harder the block will become. Your best course is to let it fade."

"But she..."

"Do you want that block to lobotomize her?"

Chuck's bleary eyes focused on Vincent, he shook his head.

"Then go in there and say you're sorry, it was a bad joke, and beg her to forgive you. We all know you are right. She just has to figure it out for herself."

Chuck nodded. Vincent let him go and he went back into the apartment. Vincent stared at the wall for a moment. What was Nathan up too? Why put a block on Andi? he thought.

Vincent slammed his fist against the wall. "Fuck it."

CHAPTER 7

The following night, Vincent went downstairs to Cassie's shop. A snowstorm blew snow across the street. The snow came down in heavy flakes, not enough now to slow people down. In about an hour that would change.

Vincent opened the door. The door chime went off. Cassie came out of the back and waved to him. "Hey! Long time no see!"

"Hi Cassie," Vincent said. He leaned over to get a kiss on his cheek. Her curly, long brown hair brushed against his cheek, tickling him.

"What brings you around?" she asked.

"There was a little situation last night. With Andi."

"What happened?"

Vincent glanced around the shop. There were two other people in the store, looking over the gemstones. He motioned with his head. Cassie took him to the psychic reading room.

She shut the door behind him. Vincent sat down on the reclining couch. "You know about Nathan Stout?"

Cassie grinned. "I love his stories. And he is sort of cute."

"He's a vampire."

"He just says that."

Vincent shook his head. "No, for real."

"Oh."

He waited until the smile faded from Cassie's face. "He invited Andi over to his place, and he messed with her mind."

"What do you mean?" Cassie asked.

"He almost scrambled it."

"Is she okay?"

"Sort of. Nothing else happened to her, but she is having memory problems."

"Poor girl." Cassie bit her nail. "Is there anything I can do?"

"Not really. I just..." he turned away.

"Vince, you don't feel responsible, do you?" Cassie asked.

"A bit. I should have chased him off. But he seemed so..." Vincent waved his hands in the air. "Nice."

"Why don't you go and speak to him?" Cassie asked. "Remember when you had to take over that coked out supermodel?"

"She went crazy. There was nothing else to do."

"Maybe something like that. I know we are talking about Andi, but maybe something happened around her."

"You could be right," Vincent said. "I should speak to him. Could you give me a minute?"

Cassie nodded. She left the room. Vincent reached out with his mind and found Verina. He told her what he wanted to do.

During this storm? she asked.

Why not? Like a little snow will hurt you.

Fine, wait for me.

Vincent went out of the room and sat down at the coffee bar to wait for Verina. The two customers left. Cassie poured herself some tea.

"Thank goodness Swen is picking me up tonight," she said. Cassie motioned her head toward the window. The snow fell in a steady stream.

"How bad is it going to get?" he asked.

"About a foot, with wind."

"You can always crash at Rebecka's old apartment."

Cassie waved her hand. "Don't worry about me."

Minutes later, Verina knocked on the window. Vincent said goodbye to Cassie. He opened the door to the blowing snow. The snow came down so hard that it took a few minutes to cover a car. The wind blew the snow into small whirlwinds of white.

"Why is this so important?" Verina asked.

"Because he tried to fry Andi's mind. No one messes with my donors," Vincent said.

"Like old times," she said.

The wind blew against them. They misted and used the blowing snow to cover their movements. Vincent slid ahead of Verina. He had gotten the address from Chuck the night before.

He found the place. Vincent and Verina solidified outside a condo building. The tall glass structure dominated the block. It looked like a crystal flame against the rectangular buildings that surrounded it. Vincent hit the buzzer for Nathan's condo.

"Mr. Hugh, what are you doing here?" Nathan asked.

"Just a visit."

"I'll send Harry down."

Verina patted her arms to knock off the snow. "He's letting us in?"

Vincent nodded.

"Either an idiot or we shouldn't mess with him," Verina said.

Vincent shrugged. Harry came across the entryway and opened the door for them. They followed him to the elevator. The building had security on every floor. The rich always wanted to have excess security. They could afford it. Vincent knew from experience. No matter how good your security was, someone could always get through.

The elevator opened to a large entry hall on the tenth floor. Harry led them across the entryway and opened the door with a key card.

Nathan stood up as they entered. "I did not expect visitors on such a cold night."

He waved them down to his sunken living room. A computer sat off to the side, covered with yellow sticky notes. One side of the living room had floor-to-ceiling windows, the view of the city would have been impressive, but only the blowing snow could be seen. The wind hit the windows and rattled them. Nathan nodded to Harry. He left.

Vincent and Verina walked down the steps to his living room. Nathan stood up and took their jackets. He placed them on an end table next to his computer.

"Andi was here," Vincent said.

"Yes, she was. She has some delightful friends," Nathan said. He went back to the couch and sat down. He motioned to the other seats.

"Good," Vincent said. "Then why did you put a block on her memories?"

Nathan picked a piece of lint off his slacks. "Because that damned werewolf had no manners."

Verina sat down. Vincent did not.

"Tell me what happened," he said.

"It was a nice evening," Nathan said. "I invited Andi and her friends here. We had a light dinner. Nothing fancy, just some fish and vegetables. Of course I declined to join them." Nathan chuckled.

"I had bought some wine. That boy Chuck? He drank more than his share," Nathan said. "The girls wanted to talk about my books, especially the new one that I am working on. Chuck got belligerent. He made some comments that were not befitting a young man. Andi was hurt. So we tricked him into leaving. I wanted to make sure Andi remembered she had a good time."

"She forgot she was even here."

Verina crossed her legs, pulling down her short skirt at the same time. She patted the seat next to her. Vincent shook his head.

Nathan maintain his smile. "Oh. Well you know it is not a precise science. I must have made a mistake, that's all. It should wear off in a few days."

"So Chuck was a jerk?" Vincent asked.

Nathan nodded. Verina tugged Vincent's shirt. He sat down. He tried to scan Nathan's mind. He blocked every move Vincent made.

He would not be able to read if Nathan was lying or not.

A soft noise came from a room off to the side. Vincent glanced over. A young woman stood in the open door way. She wore a little robe and nothing else.

Nathan waved her over. “Have you met Janice? She is one of Andi's friends.”

Janice walked over to Nathan and sat down next to him. Her eyes were cloudy and unfocused. She was under a thrall. Verina caught Vincent's eye. Her lip curled up on one side.

“Say hello, Janice,” Nathan said.

“Hi,” she said. Her voice sounded flat.

“What are you doing?” Vincent asked.

“She is just a little distraction,” Nathan said. He stroked the side of her neck. “Janice stayed after everyone left. You should have seen the fantasies in her mind. They would have made me blush, if I were still human.”

Verina shifted in her seat. Her eyes narrowed, and she glared at him. If looks could kill, Nathan would have burned up in an instant.

“Why are you controlling her, then?” Verina asked. “I thought most of your fans wanted to open their legs for you.”

“You have been hanging out with musicians too long,” Nathan said. “She wanted to, but was too modest. I just dropped the barriers, that's all. You should try her blood. It has a slight spicy taste to it.”

Nathan patted Janice's knee. She stood up. Vincent glanced at Verina. Through her narrowed eyelids, her eyes glowed red. Vincent saw Nathan's grin widen. He's making a challenge, Vincent thought. If I don't, he's won this round. Vincent nodded.

Nathan snapped his fingers. Janice walked over to Vincent and took off her robe. The welts from Nathan's bites covered her body. She had them on her breasts, stomach, and thighs. Vincent took an arm and bit her wrist. He caught Verina's eye. She looked away.

Vincent only took a little blood. It was spicy, but weak. Nathan had almost drained her already. She had deep shadows under her eyes. Her skin had turned a deep olive tinge. She has a week, Vincent thought, if he keeps feeding on her like this.

Verina snapped open her handbag. “So you gonna drain her?” she asked, taking out a black metal cigarette case. “What a way to show support for your fan."

"Please, there is no smoking in this building," Nathan said. Janice returned to her seat next to Nathan. She hadn't bothered to pick up her robe.

Verina closed the case with a quick slap of the metal. She shoved it back into her handbag, never taking her eyes off Nathan.

Nathan stroked Janice's hair, like she was a pet. "No, I won't drain her. In a few days, I will let her rest. Order out some good food and get her healthy. Then let her go home." He smiled. "Why would I kill her? I need every book sale."

He leaned forward and picked up the robe. "Janice, wait for me."

Janice put on the robe and went back to the side room. The door opened. Vincent caught a whiff of some of the smells. There was blood, and the musky smell of human sex. But there was something else. He had smelled it before, a long time ago.

"I am sorry about Andi," Nathan said. "I get a little over zealous sometimes."

Verina patted her handbag. Her cell phone rang.

Vincent put on his best smile. "I can totally understand."

"We have to go," Verina said, throwing her cell phone back in her purse. "Thank you for your time, Mr. Stout."

"Please, call me Nathan."

Verina looked at him with a blank expression for a moment. "No, I think not."

Vincent grabbed their coats. He tried to say something to Verina, but she placed her finger to her lips. It wasn't until they were a few blocks away that she did say something.

"What an asshole." She lit a cigarette; the end glowed red in the wind. "What the hell does he think he is getting away with?"

"I know, playing with his food like that," Vincent said.

"You do the same."

"I do not."

"Yes, you do," Verina said. She pointed her long fingernail at Vincent. "You take them in your little room, give them a good fantasy and have your fill. The only difference is at least yours make it home every night."

"What about you?"

"What about me?"

"Toby?"

"That's different."

"Is it?"

"He knows. You make them forget. Nathan controls them. We are all playing the same game. Some just play harder."

Vincent opened his mouth to argue, but she was right. Nathan was the same, but on a grander scale. "Okay, fine," he said.

Verina gave him a sorry look. "But you don't make them a fuck toy either."

"You smelled it too?"

"The girl was reeking," she said. "I bet it's that man, Harry. Probably his little payment for keeping his mouth shut."

Vincent shook his head. "Why do it like that? It's too risky. If Nathan screws up on the thrall and she wakes up, what then?"

"Slit her throat?"

Vincent waited until a squall subsided. Verina gave up smoking and put the cigarette out on the heel of her boot. Vincent shook his head. "He's sloppy."

"I agree. He has found his way to survive. I don't like it, but then he would say my way is horrible too."

"I couldn't tell if he was lying."

"He was," she said, pulling her fur-lined hood over her head.

"How did you know?" he asked.

"I can tell. You don't have to read minds to tell when someone is lying. It's easier with humans; their heart rate changes. But with him? That story was too well thought out."

Vincent growled. "He should have left Andi alone."

"Agreed. He should have known better." She looked at her watch. "I should get back."

Vincent nodded. Verina ran one of her hardened fingernails down his cheek and smiled. "See you soon."

The wind blew, swirling the snow. Verina disappeared as the snow danced around. Vincent faded into shadow, heading back toward the Rathskeller. He took the long way so he could think.

I play with my food? he thought. I never force myself on any of the women. I do put on the glamor, but I never forced them. I might use a thrall, but that was to dull the pain when I drink. They come into the room willingly. They leave the room and go on with their lives.

Vincent paused. He watched the blinking light of a neon sign for a moment, while he settled his thoughts. A couple of times I could have repeat meals, he thought. But, donors were better. They knew what they were giving up.

The thrall was tricky. Vincent didn't know if Nathan forced Janice to stay. How long could he keep that up? Putting a person in a thrall took a lot of effort. You had to be a puppet master, controlling them while making sure you did not forget who you were.

The mind block was another risk. Vincent hadn't lied to Chuck when he had said it could lobotomize Andi. An overpowering block and the mind became scrambled. He had done it once. The young man followed Vincent around like a modern movie zombie. The brain-dead vassal would do anything you wanted them to do. But they had to be taken care of. The one Vincent had fried would not eat, even with food in front of him, without Vincent telling him to. Vincent had to kill him a few days later.

Vincent flipped up the lapels on his jacket and walked into the wind. The night Andi went over to Nathan's, he must not have expected her to bring Chuck. Nathan did not want Chuck there. A werewolf would not be affected by a thrall.

If Vincent had been in the same situation, he would want to get the werewolf out of there, just like Nathan had done. The thrall he put on Andi did two things: made her forget about Chuck and Janice. He had messed with Andi and Janice's heads, but only kept Janice there.

Vincent stood outside the Rathskeller, the snow came down like sheets of white feathers. He walked to the back of the building. As he opened the door, sweeping the snow off the top step, Vincent paused. Something was wrong. He slammed the door and jumped to the patio outside of John and Lorelei's apartment.

John paced back and forth with his cell phone in his hand. He turned around and opened the patio door. The top of Lorelei's head could be seen over the edge of the couch. Her blue hair turned a green hue in the lights.

"Yeah, yeah, if you see him have him call," John said into his cell phone. He pointed to the couch. "It's Andi."

Vincent went over to the couch. Lorelei sat on the couch with Andi's head in her lap. Andi cried, her whole body shaking.

“She forgot where she lives,” Lorelei said. “She remembered this place.”

Andi glanced up at Vincent. Her teary eyes focus and unfocused on his face. “Who are you?” she asked.

Vincent tried to read her mind. The block had grown.

“Who were you calling?” he asked John.

“Chuck,” John said. “She remembers Chuck.”

Vincent watched the falling snow. What was happening to Andi should not be happening. Damn that Nathan. He reached out to Verina again.

Verina, Andi is starting to forget random things.

That asshole.

I don't think I can help her. Vincent laid his arm against the glass, then his head against his arm.

There used to be vampire in town that had been a doctor, but I am sure he has moved on.

Who?

Ogden Phelps.

Vincent left the apartment. The words, “I will be back,” had not left his lips when he jumped off the patio. He had only seen Ogden once, since they had moved the Coiree to its new resting spot. That had been a chance meeting. Ogden stopped his car and told Vincent to come by sometime. Better late than never, Vincent thought.

Ogden's mansion sat in the snow covered lawn like a Christmas painting. Vincent solidified at the front door and rang the bell. He almost rang it again when it was opened by a slender, dark-haired woman.

Another Hindu, Vincent noticed. She was dressed in a feminine cut business suit, her hair pulled back in a long braid. She did not smile or show any emotion as she opened the door.

“I need to see Ogden,” Vincent said.

“He is indisposed,” she said. Her voice had a slight accent. Boston? Vincent thought.

“Tell him Vincent is here.”

“Anula,” Ogden's voice rang from the top of the entry hall. “He is an old friend. Let him in.”

Anula stepped away from the door. She watched Vincent enter the hall. Shutting the door behind him with a sharp click. Ogden stood at the top of the stairs.

He motioned to Vincent. “Come up.”

Anula picked up a briefcase by the door and walked across the hall, ignoring Vincent. He climbed the stairs, feeling like he was under-dressed. Ogden waited for him at the top and opened a door.

Vincent entered the room. It was a large, semi-circular library. The cabinets were filled with books, most of them with hand-written titles. The old leather-bound volumes weighed the place down. Not just by the amount in the room, but the size of the tomes as well. At one end of the large library sat a table surrounded by a few cushion chairs. Ogden sat at one side of the table and motioned Vincent to sit at the other.

“This is a pleasant surprise,” Ogden said. “I take it this is not a social call.”

Vincent told Ogden everything, except that Chuck was a werewolf. Ogden listened, his fingers steepled before him on the table.

When Vincent had finished, all Ogden said was, “Hm.”

“Well?” Vincent asked.

“Mr. Stout has no manners,” Ogden said. By the look on his face he was still trying to sort out everything Vincent had said. “And his writing style is almost childish.”

“You've read his books?”

“I stay current with all the fiction about our kind, a guilty hobby of mine.”

Ogden stood up, straightened out his smoking jacket, and walked over to a bookcase that held the modern books. He pulled out *Ashes at Dawn*.

“The cover is interesting,” Ogden said, handing the book to Vincent. On the cover was a forlorn looking dark-haired man holding a woman close to him. The painting was done like every romance novel Vincent had seen. Except in this one, the woman was not looking up to the man with lust in her eyes. Her eyes were closed, giving the appearance of her sleeping or that she was dead. The couple stood in a graveyard.

“Of all of them, that is the most original of the series,” Ogden said. “The main character is a vampire named Stephan Ashington. Supposedly an old English lord, but that is one of the biggest works of fiction in this story. He had become a vampire during the reign of Elizabeth the First. He lives fine for a few centuries until he mets a woman named Angelica." Ogden paused and rolled his eyes. "Then it turns into a horrible romance. He wants to change for her. She gives herself willingly to him. She ends up dead at the end. There are two chapters at the end that deal with his mourning her death."

"Sounds dreadful," Vincent said.

Ogden grinned. His fangs just peeking out of the corners of his mouth. "When this book first came out, no one had read it. I think I was one of the first. They did not become popular until some talk show host suggested it for some light reading."

He sat back down. "That is one of the first editions. It might be worth something in a few decades. Look at the book jacket."

Vincent opened it up to the photograph of Nathan. This was not the Nathan that Vincent had met. Gone were the Victorian clothes and the close-shaved beard. Here, he looked more like a poet in the style of Lord Byron.

"He told me he never had any pictures taken," Vincent said.

"Later editions that is true," Ogden said. "I found it interesting that the more his books became popular the more he didn't lie about what he was."

"You knew?"

"All stories have a pinch of truth," Ogden said. "But the biggest clue for me was his description of some of the military campaigns the main character had been on. There was one in particular that sounded very familiar to me. Just a small skirmish with the Thuggees in India."

Ogden motioned for the book, Vincent handed it over. Ogden opened the book. He read.

"We went out on that humid, heat sickening day, looking for the vandals that were attacking travelers for their heathen goddess. The officer in command, an arrogant aristocrat named Major Ogden Phelps, led us into the god-forsaken jungle. I did not know what was the bigger danger, the tigers that watched us with hungry, hazel eyes, or the dark heathens with their plans of murder for a false goddess."

Ogden paused. "He goes on and on like that. The thing is, I was a major in India. We did go into the jungle to find the Thuggees."

"Are you sure?"

Ogden nodded. “He gives details that did not appear on any official reports. I think I remember him. But he was not a vampire then.”

“Who was he?” Vincent asked.

“A frustrated journalist.” Ogden waved his hand in a dismissive gesture. “Old history. But your friend, she is the one that needs help now.”

Ogden stood up and walked to the blackened windows, he stood there a moment in thought. Then he turned around, rubbing his chin. “There maybe a way. If you can get her to come here tomorrow, I will try to do my best.”

Vincent nodded. He stood up to leave and felt the stupor start to take him. Dawn was coming now? He leaned on the chair, fighting the exhaustion.

“I will show you to a room,” Ogden said.

He led Vincent to a small room with no windows. The bed had an ornate iron frame around it. The stupor overtook Vincent. He fell into the bed. He heard Ogden close the door, then nothing.

CHAPTER 8

Vincent opened his eyes, saw the paisley comforter and almost didn't remember where he was. He rolled over on the bed and sat up. He could hear a heartbeat outside the room. He got up, stretched, and opened the door. Anula sat across the hall from him.

"Ogden wanted me to make sure you meet him in the parlor," she said, standing up from the red velvet covered chair. "I'll show you."

Anula led him down the hall and down the stairs. She opened a set of double doors, standing aside to let him enter. The room looked as if it came right out of a Victorian upper class home. The chairs were arranged in a way that conversations would flow easily. There were curio cabinets and photographs along the walls. A set of large French doors led to a garden, which was covered in a thick blanket of snow, except were someone had cleared the pathway.

She closed the door behind him. Vincent went over to the photos. The oldest ones were black and white. The poses were stiff. Vincent remembered those, having to stand perfectly still while the film was exposed. He found a couple of photos of Ogden. He was dressed in a British military uniform.

A larger one, in a gold frame, was Ogden standing behind a beautiful Hindu woman. She was dressed in an ornate black gown. Vincent recognized the type of photo, a wedding photo. He grinned. Next to it were a couple of photos of children.

Vincent looked at the faces, all staring back at him. All of them had the same chin, the same eyes, and the same black hair. Vincent realized he was looking at Ogden's family.

The photos became more informal as they became more modern. In a digital picture frame were some candid shots of Anula and Manas. In one they were sitting with an older gentleman. Anula was dressed in a graduation gown and a mortarboard hat.

"Sorry I am late," Ogden said from the doorway. "I was arranging a meal for us."

Vincent pointed to the photos. "Your family?"

Ogden nodded. "Another hobby of mine."

He turned away and motioned to a phone. "Make the arrangements you need to. Tell them I have already sent Manas over."

Vincent called John. Andi was still at their apartment. He told John to bring her over to Ogden's, but to wait for Manas. He had just hung up when the door opened.

Two women stood in the doorway. They had not dressed for the weather: both of them wore short skirts and halter tops. Vincent rubbed his goatee and smiled. They were call girls.

"This is my friend Vincent," Ogden said. "Vincent, this is Dawn and Lindsey."

Dawn had a full face and blond hair permed into ringlets. Lindsey had short brunette hair and stood taller than Dawn.

"These two are my favorites," Ogden said. "Be nice."

Vincent could hear the threat with the words 'be nice.' Dawn grabbed Ogden's hand. They went to the other side of the room, giving Vincent and Lindsey some privacy. Lindsey removed the choker around her neck.

"Are you sure you want it on the neck?" Vincent asked.

She stared at him, like he was from another planet. Vincent drew her to him and bit her neck. Her body stiffened for a moment, then relaxed. He fed enough to last through the night. When he finished, Lindsey put her choker back on.

The room was quiet. He felt like he needed to make some conversation. "You don't mind this?" Vincent asked.

"I wouldn't do what I do if I minded it," she said. "Besides, he pays well. There are worse things he could ask us to do."

Dawn came over, adjusting the bodice of her dress. Ogden followed. "There is dinner waiting for you in the dining room," he told the women. "Manas will take both of you out later."

The women left. Ogden shrugged. "It's the price we pay..."

"I've paid for them, too," Vincent said. "Although, the ones I used worked the side streets."

Ogden smirked then motioned to the couch. "Can you assist me in getting the room ready?"

"Ready for what?" Vincent asked.

"For your friend. I have asked one of my relations to come and help as well. I think we should start by moving the couch."

Vincent helped Ogden move the furniture. As he slid the heavy oak table to the wall, the door opened. A gray-haired, heavy set man walked in, carrying a black bag. Vincent recognized the man, he had seen him in the photographs on the wall.

Ogden greeted him. "Thank you for coming. Lawrence, I want you to meet my friend, Vincent."

Lawrence nodded to Vincent. "You want me to monitor her vitals, correct?"

Ogden nodded. "What I think needs to be done could shut her brain down."

"Wait," Vincent said. "Brain dead? Are you sure you can help her?"

"I have to see what was done first. Then I will try my best."

Lawrence placed his bag on a table and took out his supplies: a stethoscope, blood pressure cuff, and a small box about the size of a CD player. He opened the box. It looked like an oscillator.

"When this finally goes into production," Lawrence said, turning the box on, "every hospital is going to want one."

"Is that the vital signs monitor?" Ogden asked.

"Yes." Lawrence nodded. "As long as it is placed within ten feet of this sensor." He held up a small disk. "It can read all the vitals wirelessly and send the information to a central server."

The doorbell rang somewhere in the house. Ogden left the room for a moment.

"So you are related to Ogden?" Vincent asked.

Lawrence nodded. "I forgot how many greats, but I am a direct descendant."

"Really?"

Lawrence handed Vincent a long slender rod. "Put that on the table, please."

"What's this?"

"A defibrillator."

"Aren't they usually paddles?"

Lawrence nodded. "It's another prototype. I hope I don't have to use it."

Ogden returned. Behind him came John and Chuck. Chuck helped Andi into the room. She rested her head on Chuck's shoulder.

"Place her on the couch, please," Ogden said.

Chuck helped her lay down. Ogden went over and stood at the end of the couch, next to her head.

"Chuck..." Andi said.

Chuck took her hand. "I don't know if I should stay," he said.

"Stay," Ogden said.

Chuck sat down on the floor, not letting go of Andi's hand. Lawrence came over to the couch and laid the disc on Andi's chest.

John stood next to Vincent. "She woke up this afternoon very confused," he said in a low tone. "She keeps hearing a voice."

Ogden placed his fingers on the side of her head and closed his eyes. Moments passed. The monitor beeped quietly. Ogden twitched.

"This is not just a block," he said. "There is a thrall as well. Impressive."

The monitor beeped. Lawrence took Andi's other hand to take her pulse. She squeezed Chuck's hand.

Ogden moved his finger tips around her head. “He's good.”
John leaned closer to Vincent. “I hope he knows what he is doing.”
Vincent nodded. “I hope so too.”
Then he felt it, a stabbing pain in his mind. At the same time, Andi cried out and Ogden winced. Ogden moved his fingers. The pain intensified, Vincent pinched his forehead. He could feel Nathan in his head. Vincent grunted. Nathan fought back.
Ogden's fingertips turned white. Andi moaned. The beeping on the monitor picked up tempo.
Lawrence read the screen. “Her brain activity is off the charts.”
Vincent found the part of his brain where the pain intensified. He followed it out of his mind. Nathan used Andi as a focal point. His attacks on Vincent were coming from her. Vincent touched Ogden's mind.
Ogden blocked Nathan's attack. Vincent had to jump back to his and stop a simultaneous attack. He blocked Nathan from burning his brain. But then he felt Nathan try to move around to Ogden using Andi's mind.
Vincent pinched his forehead harder and shot back at Nathan. Nathan weakened for a moment. Ogden moved in. Vincent felt the block dropping from Andi's mind. Vincent opened his eyes. Andi's nose bled. Her hand gripped Chuck's hand so hard that his had turned white.
“Vincent,” Ogden said, forcing the word out. “If you would be so kind to make sure he does not come back.”
Vincent closed his eyes. Nathan came back for another attack. Vincent blocked him. He felt Ogden move in the background. Nathan hit Vincent hard. It felt like his brain had an ice pick shoved into it.
“Vince,” John whispered. “You're bleeding.”
Vincent rubbed his face. He smeared the blood from his nose and eyes across his hand.
“Damn that Nathan.” Vincent absorbed the blood back into his body. He shot back at Nathan so hard he threw his body forward with the force.
“Her brain waves are crashing,” Lawrence said.
“Put her to sleep,” Ogden said.
Lawrence prepared a needle.

"No! Don't!" Andi squirmed away from Lawrence.
"Andi, hon, calm down," Chuck said.
"I don't like needles!"
Chuck kissed Andi. "Sweety, they have to put you asleep."
"I don't-"
"Andi, please."
Lawrence injected the needle into Andi. Her eyes fluttered. Chuck stroked her cheek until she fell asleep.
Vincent felt Nathan lose his anchor. Ogden moved in. Andi had been fighting him too. Vincent could put Andi in a thrall; she did not know how to fight back. It had to be part of the thrall that Nathan had put on her. He felt Ogden push around the thrall. It disappeared from her mind.
Ogden stood back. "I've done all I can."
Vincent wiped his face. His nose bled again. Ogden walked over to one of the side tables and wiped his face. He had blood flowing from his eyes and nose as well.
"He is very strong," Vincent said.
Ogden nodded.
Chuck placed Andi's hand on her chest. "So is that it?" Chuck asked.
"Yes, keep her away from him," Ogden said. "He wanted a way into her head. He found it."
"That bastard's dead," Chuck said.
"Oh, no, not yet," Ogden said. "He has strong mental powers. He would even find away around your defenses."
"How?"
"He was controlling Andi and Janice at the same time."
Chuck looked surprised. "Janice? How did he get a hold of her?"
"When you were over there," Vincent said.
"No, she left."
"She was in the pictures you showed us," Vincent said.
"No she wasn't."
Ogden walked over to Chuck and raised his hand. "May I?" He asked.
Chuck bowed his head toward Ogden. It took a moment. "He blocked you too? But not a hard one to drop."
Chuck stood still for a moment. "Oh God!"
"What happened?" Vincent asked.

“Janice did come with us,” Chuck said. “We had dinner. Something he had ordered out. Janice excused herself to used the bathroom. Nathan excused himself, to get a book, he said. But Janice never came back. He told us that it was a pity she never came. We believed him.”

Chuck looked down. “I was an idiot. I think the wine was drugged. I remember feeling a little light-headed.”

“You drank nearly a case of beer before you started to slur,” John said.

“I know. Normally, I don't drink, it just doesn't do anything to me. But I did pass out that night.”

“So he might be using drugs, too,” Ogden said. He motioned to Lawrence. They went to the side of the room and had a private conversation.

“Nathan is a real asshole,” said Chuck.

“He's good,” Vincent said. “He covers his tracks well, as long as he is not covering them around other vampires and werewolves.”

“Thank the gods they are finishing up the filming tonight,” John said. “'Cause I don't know if I want that guy anywhere near the club.”

“Good thing if he comes by the club,” Vincent said with a wicked grin. “He will have to deal with Swen.”

John chuckled.

Ogden came back. “Why don't you take Andi home?” Ogden said to John and Chuck. “Vincent, I need to speak to you privately.”

They went out into the hall. “This Nathan could be very dangerous,” Ogden said. “It took two of us plus a sedative to undo his damage.”

“He still has Andi's roommate,” Vincent said.

“She is probably dead already.”

Vincent opened his mouth to argue.

Ogden leaned closer. “You said yourself she was close to death. Nathan knows it was you fighting him. He might even figure out it was me. But for now, you must protect the ones close to you.”

“You said you knew him,” Vincent said.

“I think so,” Ogden nodded.

“Was he an ass, then?”

“He tried too hard. But he was a fastidious observer. He knew how the human mind worked even then. If psychology had been a discipline at that time, he would have been an excellent practitioner. There are not many vampires that can be that strong with their minds. You and I are unusual. That is why we have such control. But the bloodline that he may have come from is rare."

"So you want me to find the one that made him?" Vincent asked. "That is nearly impossible."

"No, but just remember we might not know all that he can do," Ogden said. "Manas will be taking our earlier guests out to the clubs or some such thing. I will have Lawrence take you home. Besides, he can make sure Andi is all right, physically."

"Is he a doctor?" Vincent asked.

"Was. Now, he develops medical equipment."

They went back into the room. Chuck picked up Andi, who was still asleep, like a child.

John shook his head. "I don't think we should take Andi home."

"Why not?" Ogden asked.

"Because Nathan got into her roommate's head. He could figure out how to get a hold of Andi again."

"Good point," Ogden said.

"Rebecka's old apartment is empty," Vincent said.

"Lawrence, go with them, please," Ogden said.

They left Ogden's house. They didn't take the Bentley that Ogden usually used. Lawrence drove a minivan, with John in the passenger seat. Vincent sat in the middle. Chuck sat in the back with Andi sleeping on the seat. Vincent rubbed his head.

His head felt like he had been on an all-night drinking spree. The pain radiated out from where Nathan had fought back. A thrall did not feel like that. He had not felt anything like that in a long time. When he had been a prisoner of Joshua's, he had felt something similar.

When Verina had broken him out of his cage, his head had become clear for the first time. For a day afterward, his head felt like this. But not as strong. Vincent rubbed his temple. The pain hit him deep in his brain.

Andi moaned in her sleep. Vincent caught a glimpse of Chuck stroking her cheek. The only way Nathan could get into the werewolf's head was by using drugs. Did he know Chuck was coming too?

“Chuck,” Vincent said. He didn't turn his head. “Did Nathan know you were coming along?”

“No, Andi never told him who was coming.”

“Okay. So why did he have the drugs?” Vincent turned in his seat to look at Chuck.

“Maybe they belong to Harry.” Chuck leaned forward. “He smells strange.”

“He has sex with Nathan's victims.”

John turned around in the front seat. “When they are dead?”

“I wouldn't put it past him.”

“Sicko.”

Lawrence coughed. “A necrophiliac? It would make sense, they often find employment where they will have access to corpses.”

“Hey,” Chuck said. “Andi's friend is still there.”

“She was almost dead last night,” Vincent said. “I doubt she's alive now.”

“Couldn't you do anything?”

Vincent turned in his seat and growled. “What would you have done?”

“Vince,” John said.

“There are rules we follow,” Vincent said. “Attacking a vampire in his home is almost suicide.”

“What do you mean almost?” Chuck asked.

“Do you think I would let anyone wander into my apartment?”

“How did you get in?”

Vincent pinched the bridge of his nose. “He invited me in.”

How could Nathan have been so arrogant? Vincent thought. Everyone who worked at the Rathskeller was under Vincent's protection. You did not touch the humans who were watched over by another vampire. Even when Vincent had escaped his servitude, he knew that rule.

“He came into the Rathskeller,” Vincent said. His voice snarled. “He knew who was under my protection and he still messed with them.”

“And you let him get away with it,” Chuck said.

Vincent spun around in his seat, raising his hand to strike Chuck.

Chuck looked down at Andi. “We both messed up. I should have protected her better.”

Vincent lowered his hand. Chuck glanced up at Vincent, his eyes had turned yellow and his teeth had grown longer. He stroked Andi's cheek. "But she wouldn't listen to us, either."

John cleared his throat. "Neither of you messed up," he said. "Both of you were suckered in like all of us were. Whatever he does, he does it well. The thing is, you know about it now. You didn't before."

"How were you suckered in?" Vincent asked.

"I thought he was like you."

Vincent sat back on the seat. He watched the city pass by them. Like me, he thought. How could John think that?

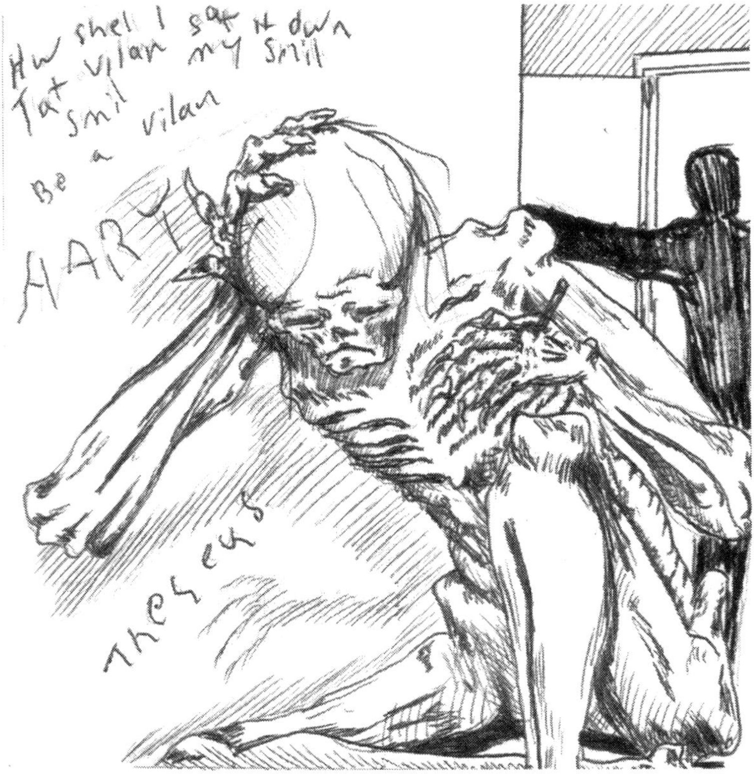

CHAPTER 9

The next evening, Vincent knocked on the door to Rebecka's old apartment. Chuck opened it. Andi ran out and tackled Vincent with a hug. He stumbled back across the hallway.

"Thank you," she said, kissing his cheek.

Vincent struggled to get away. "You're welcome," he said, laughing.

Andi pulled Vincent inside. He hit the barrier as she pulled him through the door frame. She giggled. "Sorry, come in."

He stepped over a pile of empty pizza boxes. Chuck leaned against the kitchen counter. "Yeah, thanks," he said.

"How are you doing?" Vincent asked.

"It feels like I woke up to a great day," Andi said. "And I was starving."

"Four pizzas," Chuck said.

"You had some too. I'll probably puke later, but it was worth it." Andi squeezed Vincent's arm. Her hair was damp; he could smell the shampoo and conditioner. A small dab of soap suds hung under her right ear.

"I called my roommates; that was awkward," she said. "The cops wanted to talk to me about Janice disappearing. Guess who they sent over?"

"No idea," Vincent said.

"Grady! Swen's buddy. I was so relieved. I could tell him the whole truth."

"I couldn't believe it when she started telling him about Nathan being a vampire," Chuck said.

"But I didn't say anything about you." Andi pointed at Chuck. "I didn't want your dad mad at me."

"Do you think she is still alive?" Chuck asked. The look on his face told Vincent that he didn't think so.

"I'm not sure," Vincent said.

"You have to go get Janice," Andi said.

Vincent pried Andi's fingers from his arm. "I don't know if that is a good idea."

"Vincent, please, it's my fault she's there." Her eyes watered.

"Look, Andi, about that..."

"No, no, no, no. Not you too," she said.

"I've already told her no," Chuck said.

"I can't believe you two. You're acting all scared."

"I am not scared of him," Vincent said. "He knows I know what he did. If I go there now, he will try to kill me."

"Sounds like you're scared," Andi said. She sat on the couch, with her arms crossed.

Chuck went over to her. "Andi, you know I asked my brothers to help. Let them get back to me first."

"She could be dead by then."

Vincent went to the door. He waved at them. "We'll discuss this later."

He slipped out the door before Andi could protest. He hurried down the hall. The door to John and Lorelei's apartment was open.

He went inside. Swen and John stood in the dining area, talking.

"How's Andi?" Swen asked.

"Better, except she wants me and/or Chuck to go save Janice," Vincent said.

"You think she is dead?"

Vincent nodded.

"Then I think you should make Andi think you at least tried."

"Explain."

"Back in Kuwait, I saw this guy get ripped apart by a mini gun. We knew he was dead. But his buddy refused to believe it. Our medic pretended to try to save him. It was more for show than for a miracle."

"So you want me to disappear for a few hours, come back and say she's dead?" Vincent scoffed. "That's cold."

"Well, what do you want to do?" John asked.

"Kill Nathan."

For a moment, the refrigerator running in the kitchen was the only sound in the apartment.

Swen rubbed his beard. "Do you want my blood tonight?"

Vincent shook his head and backed away. "No! That one time was enough."

Swen chuckled. "Yeah, that's right."

"Do you think Nathan is still around?" John asked.

"We have two people down the hall that can prove he's a killer," Vincent said. "I think he will want to stick around. To try to mess with them."

John nodded. He rolled up his sleeve. "Let's make this quick."

Vincent had his meal, then went outside to try to get his head together. The crisp air felt good on his skin. The clouds hung low, ready to dump a few more inches of snow on the ground.

He started to reach out with his mind for Verina, but stopped. He felt Nathan, lurking on the edge. Vincent blocked his mind from any vampire looking for him. He could feel Nathan searching through the city.

Vincent paused by a corner bar. From the sounds that echoed out when the door opened, there were a lot of people inside. Vincent walked in. He had to step aside immediately, or would have had a middle-aged woman knock him over. Inside, most of the patrons were sitting around the small darkened stage.

He glanced over the crowd. It was a blue collar type of place. Posters of women holding beers or tools lined the walls, the jukebox played classic 70's rock, and the only neon lights were the beer signs. Most of the men looked as if they had just came off their shift at a garage. Not many women wore dresses. Everyone seemed to be wearing jeans. Vincent fit in.

When he was human, he would have been a regular at a place like this, although when he was alive, his buddies and him would go down to the river and drink whatever they could get their hands on. This place did not look like a rough bar, but any place could become one with the right mix of alcohol and stupidity.

The bartender came up to Vincent. He ordered a beer. A beer was a safe bet. If you started ordering any drinks fancier than "rum and coke." you would get strange looks. The bartender came back sliding the beer glass over. Vincent laid a ten dollar bill down on the bar. The bartender took it without giving Vincent another look.

Vincent assumed the posture of slow drinker. He kept his shoulders slouched over the bar, arms held close to his sides, but resting on the bar. He felt out with his mind. Nathan still looked for him. Vincent pulled back into his mind, but it was too late.

Nathan's mind started to feel out the people at the bar. He began at the back, touching each person as he moved to the front. The heavy crowd around the stage gave Nathan trouble. Vincent could feel Nathan's confusion with so many minds in one place.

This is odd, Vincent thought. Nathan has to look for me. I just have to think of his name and I can find him.

Nathan either could not reach out that way, or did not want Vincent to know he was looking. Vincent pushed the unfinished beer away and walked out of the bar. It would take Nathan a few more minutes to check everyone inside. Vincent had to get ahead of his scan.

Vincent glanced in the direction of Nathan's condo. The fool had already invited him in; there would be nothing stopping him now. He would have to sneak in. Even with all the cameras and security in place, it would not be hard. Vincent had spent twenty years getting into people's homes without them knowing.

Vincent changed into mist. He traveled faster through the city this way. He made it to the condo building, but stayed in mist form. He flowed around to the back of the building. The tenants parked in an underground parking garage. Vincent drifted in. A car pulled in behind him. Vincent floated to the ceiling and watched.

An older woman got out of the car. She went to the trunk and pulled out three grocery bags. Between her purse, which kept falling off her shoulder, and the three bags, she was not paying attention. Vincent flowed behind her.

She struggled with the bags, stopped to set the alarm on her car, then walked to the elevator. A grocery bag slipped in her hands. She caught it with her thigh. She put the key inside the lock to the elevator controls. When the door slid opened, she walked in and Vincent drifted along the floor.

She pressed a button and stood back. Vincent touched her mind. Her mind jumped from one idea to another; she thought about work, her home life, her love life, and how old she was. Vincent moved in and put her under the thrall.

She reached over and pressed the button to Nathan's floor. The elevator rose higher. It stopped. The doors opened. She got off. Vincent did not solidify. He stayed in the mist form and waited for the door to open again. He flowed out of the elevator and up into the air ducts.

He found Nathan's apartment. Below him, Harry sat cross-legged on the couch. He watched Nathan. Nathan sat across from Harry in the living room on an easy chair with his eyes closed. Nathan's one hand rested on a side table, holding a pencil. His hand moved over a map, drawing a thin line. It was the route Vincent had taken to get to the condo.

He would only have a few moments to act. He moved down the air shaft and into another part of the apartment. He found Janice, dead, her body draped over a bed, tossed on it like a piece of dirty laundry. He could not do a damn thing for her now. Vincent moved to another room.

He flowed down into the bathroom and solidified. He didn't have any time to waste. Vincent extended his claws and fangs. He slammed through the door and rushed out.

Harry started to get out of his seat. Vincent hit him and sent crashing through the furniture. Harry hit the windows and shook them harder than the wind had before. Nathan had not moved.

"Vincent," he said, with a smile. "What a surprise."

"You know it's not," Vincent said.

“It is, believe me, it is,” Nathan said. He put down his pencil with a click.

The pressure hit his head. Nathan tried to blast into Vincent's mind. Vincent fought back. His nose bled. Nathan had a small smile on his face. Vincent forced him back.

Nathan's smile had not changed. “That was good.”

“You arrogant bastard,” Vincent growled. “You came to my place and trespassed on my people.”

“Oh please,” Nathan said. “Are we still worried about territories? About who runs what parts of the city? That is so ancient.”

“It works here,” Vincent said. “I want reclamations.”

“Like what?” Nathan asked. “Money? No problem.”

Vincent felt a movement behind him. He spun around, and avoided a stake from Harry. The stake missed Vincent's chest, but hit his shoulder. Harry buried it deep, it stopped when it hit the shoulder blade. Vincent grabbed Harry's hand with one hand and with the other he pulled out the stake. He staked Harry in the same place.

Spinning back around, Vincent found an empty chair. Harry rolled on the floor. Vincent stood still. He reached out for Nathan. There was nothing but Harry moaning in pain. It had to be a block. No one disappears that well, Vincent thought.

He turned slowly in the room, sweeping the room with his mind. He felt Nathan, then the feeling was gone. Nathan was still there, but hidden. Vincent sniffed.

He smelled Nathan over the blood from Harry. Vincent swung out his claws and caught Nathan across the chest. His blood dripped off his invisible body. Vincent lunged. He caught Nathan by the neck. He slammed him against the table.

Nathan swiped Vincent across the face. His blood sprayed across the living room. He could see Nathan now. He pulled his hand back to strike him in the chest.

“You don't understand, asshole. Andi is under my protection. You fucked with her head. Not cool!” Vincent hissed.

Nathan raised his eyebrows. “Andi, she was next on my list,” he said. “Bet she would have lasted longer than her friend.”

Vincent swung Nathan around. He didn't hear Harry crying out in pain any more. Vincent glanced down. Harry was gone. A trail of blood exited the living room.

"She would have been sweet, too," Nathan said. "And that bartender of yours."

Vincent pulled Nathan closer. "You sick bastard."

He brought down his claws to tear out Nathan's heart. A pain seared across his neck. Vincent dropped to his knees, letting go of Nathan. It felt like someone was welding across his collarbone.

He clawed at his neck. His fingernails burned when he touched the thin object around his neck. Nathan stood back, smiling. Vincent clawed at him, then fell forward.

Nathan knelt beside him. "Wood, that's our real enemy. Harry just wrapped a tourniquet made of ash around your neck." Nathan chuckled. "Of course it won't choke you, but it will burn."

Vincent rolled on his side, clawing at his neck, but he could not get a grip on the ash. Harry had a longer stake in his hand. Vincent kicked at him. Harry pushed his foot away.

Nathan stood up. "Take him to Angelica."

"Are you sure?" Harry asked. "I was gonna feed her..."

Vincent felt a mind blast directed towards Harry. Harry bent over and grabbed Vincent by the tourniquet. He tugged on Vincent's neck. He couldn't fight Harry. He dragged Vincent passed the kitchen. Vincent reached up. He patted the counter as they passed, looking for something to attack with. The counter was bare. He tried to dig his claws into the woodwork. His claws could not break the finish.

Harry kicked open a back room. He shoved Vincent into the room. Vincent rolled in. Harry slammed the door shut and locked it.

Vincent scrambled to stand up. He rolled to his side and lifted his head. A hand shot out and grabbed his ankle. The hand had come out of a pile of rags. The rags shifted revealing what had been a woman. A ghoul stared at him now.

Her dark hair hung like limp strings down her face. Her dull gray eyes stared at him. Vincent kicked at her. She let out a sound like a purr. He clawed at the ash. Every time he touched it, his fingers burned. The ghoul gripped his ankle, watching him struggle. She crawled along the floor, holding him down as she sniffed her way up his body.

Vincent looked around the room for anything to hit her with. She sniffed his face, piercing his skin with her ragged claws. Vincent punched her. His fist brushed across her face. She purred.

The ghoul opened her mouth, it split in three places, and widened further than what should have been possible. The ghoul slammed her face down and tore into the flesh of his shoulder. She gnawed at the wound that the stake had left. Her tongue forced his flesh apart. He felt her teeth grab his skin and pull. Vincent wrapped his fingers in her lanky brown hair and yanked at her head.

She growled. Pieces of his skin and flesh sputtered out of her mouth. The ghoul clawed at his chest. Vincent caught her hands and slammed them against the floor. It was no use; the ash had weakened him.

The ghoul scrambled around him, sniffing and hissing. She disappeared into the darkness of the room. Vincent rolled on his side. She jumped on him again, biting his upper leg. The ghoul pulled her head back, taking a hunk of his flesh in her mouth. Vincent rolled and tried to crawl to the door. The ghoul jumped again. She dug her claws into his back and started to eat his other shoulder.

Vincent rolled, trying to dislodge the ghoul. He shoved her head off his shoulder as he rolled. She scrambled around. Vincent lifted his head, she lifted hers. They were inches apart.

The ghoul growled, opening her mouth wide. Vincent leaned back. Her mouth came down on his neck. She bit down, her teeth cutting through the ash. Pieces of the tourniquet fell to the floor. Vincent hit her head with his fists.

The burning of the ash was replaced by the pain of the ghoul tearing chunks of his neck off. Vincent cried out. The ghoul jumped off him, clawing at her mouth. She spit out a piece of the ash. Vincent rolled and jumped to his feet. The ghoul lunged at him. He grappled with her.

She growled. Her mouth split open. She clamped down on his face. This time there was no ash to repel her. She dug her teeth into his jaw. Vincent cried out. The scream muffled by her mouth.

Vincent tried turning into a mist. He couldn't. It hurt when he tried. The ghoul raised her head, pulling chunks of his flesh out.

"Bitch," Vincent stammered. He could feel that she had cut a gash from his lips to his ear. He covered the wound with his hand.

The ghoul knocked him down and continued her feeding. Vincent hit her, but she would not move. He healed, but too slowly to keep up with her hunger. He tried to shove her off again, he couldn't keep her from ripping chunks of him off.

Howling, Vincent turned his head to face the door. He thought he heard howling. The ghoul snorted. She placed her hands on the side of his face and dug her claws in.

A gunshot and more howls. Vincent heard a thud. The ghoul sniffed his face, then jerked her hands. Vincent's spine snapped.

CHAPTER 10

It felt like a dream, but he didn't dream. He recognized the room. This natural cavern had been the last thing he had seen with his human eyes. He laid on the mosaic tile of the altar that dominated the middle of the room. But he and Steopa had destroyed it, hadn't they?

Someone leaned over. The shadow blocked the view of the stone ceiling. Vincent thought he felt his heart jump. He grabbed his chest. For a moment he thought he saw his killer, Joshua.

Vincent did not feel anything move. The stillness that he was familiar with soothed his thoughts. He concentrated. The shadow lightened, but did not reveal who stood over him.

"Vincent," the figure said. "What have you gotten yourself into?"

The figure stepped closer. Wings unfolded from its back.

Vincent laughed. "An angel?"

"I supposed some would call me that. I am no angel. Daemon, perhaps, not an angel."

Vincent could not make out its features. It looked like it had long shaggy black hair. Its face was not blank, just hard to look at. Like you could not take the figure fully into your senses, only a little at a time. "So you're a grim reaper, then?"

The figure shook his head. "It doesn't matter what I am. All you need to know is that I am here."

"That makes me feel so much better."

The figure laughed.

"I'm not dead."

"Compared to humans you are." The figure smiled. Vincent could see the light glinting off his fangs. "You have been for some time, but are you destroyed? No, you are not."

The figure stepped forward. His blueish-black hair framed his pale face. Features came into focus the more Vincent concentrated. He did not look like an angel now, unless angels had more fangs than vampires did.

"A vampire?" Vincent asked.

"No, but we do share bloodlines."

"Relatives?"

"Not that simple."

Vincent turned his head away. The figure's smoky features hurt his eyes. "So what now?"

"Now you have to go back and face that vampire again."

"I screwed up. I used to be able to go in and take someone like that out in seconds." Vincent tried to look at the figure again.

"Yes, you were a magnificent killer. But do you also remember what you were like? You were not much different from the ghoul that tried to eat you."

Vincent nodded. "Like a junkyard dog, beaten and starved."

The figure tilted his head. "You are not at your full potential. You have moved beyond the killer you were. But you could be so much more."

“Like what?”

“You are a unique vampire. I know. I was here when you were made.” The figure motioned with his hand around the room. “The human did not know what he was doing when he made you. It was serendipitous.”

Vincent turned his head so he could see the doorway to the room. The figure walked into his view. He folded his wings behind his back. “You have to move beyond what you are now. You have a friend that can help you with that. She has a gift for you. Take it when she gives it to you.”

“Then what?”

“Then you will begin to reach your potential. And Nathan's death will just be the beginning.” The room faded around Vincent. The figure waved his hand. “Do your stuff.”

Vincent smelled cigarette smoke. The features of the natural cavern faded into the features of another familiar room. He waited until the room came in focus before he looked around. Verina sat cross-legged on a chair next to him. She smiled.

“You were an idiot,” she said.

Vincent tried to focus on where he was. The smell was familiar, the old smell of alcohol and formaldehyde. This was the Dysart Memorial. He could tell that he had been laying on the couch for a while. The smell of his blood was stale and old.

Verina moved her chair closer. He tried to move, but his right arm would not cooperate. His shoulder still burned where the stake had injured him. He tried moving his left arm. He could. He felt his neck. Above the scar that he knew so well was another welt, this one was from the ash.

“How?” he tried to say. His voice came out in a choking whisper.

“That werewolf that works for you,” Verina said. “He went over there too, but he was smarter. He waited until his family showed up. He left with his brothers and they waited for Nathan's vassal to leave.”

“Nathan?” Vincent asked.

“Still around, along with that ghoul. The werewolves wanted to rip him apart, but when they found you, they took you instead.” Verina stood up. “I'll go tell Rebecka and Steopa you're awake.”

Verina left. He tried to sit up. Pain hit him from many places.

Vincent laid back down and stared at the ceiling. He ran his fingers over the open wounds. His fingertips dripped with his blood. I should be a pile of ash, he thought.

Steopa loomed into view. “Good. I will take you upstairs.”

Steopa picked him up like a child. They passed Verina, who sat on one of the coffins on the middle floor. She smirked, but Vincent could see that she had been upset. Her eyes watered for a moment. She turned her head and lit a cigarette.

At the top of the memorial. Steopa laid Vincent on a pew. The Coiree sat on the old altar. Vincent swore it glowed. Rebecka picked up the Coiree and brought it over to Vincent. The insides of the Coiree sloshed. It was full of blood.

“How'd you...?” he asked.

“Just drink,” Rebecka said.

He could move his left arm, but could not hold the Coiree steady. Rebecka helped him tip the cup. The blood was warm. It had not congealed or separated. He had been expecting the flat, salty taste of old blood. This was fresh blood. Vincent felt his strength come back.

He lowered the Coiree. Rebecka returned it to the old altar.

“How many people did you-?” Vincent asked

“We didn't,” Rebecka said.

“We brought you here after Teodor and his sons did not know what to do with you,” Steopa said. “The cup filled with blood as soon as we came up here.”

“Teodor?” Vincent asked.

“Chuck's father,” Rebecka said. “Verina tried to come up here yesterday. Whatever Ogden did to this place, it kept her away.”

“You look better,” Steopa said.

Vincent wiped his face. “Wait, how long was I out?”

“A week.”

“Nathan is probably long gone,” Vincent said.

Rebecka came back over and sat down beside him. “No, in fact he is in the public more than ever.”

“Verina has been following him,” Steopa said.

“She shouldn't do that,” Vincent said. “He knows she's a friend of mine.”

“You might want to talk to her about that,” Rebecka said.

Vincent tried to stand up. He swayed on his feet. Steopa steadied

him. "You should stay up here now."
"It's not really comfortable..." Vincent said.
"Can you walk?" Steopa asked.
Vincent's knees shook, but he could put his weight on his legs without falling. Steopa hooked his arm around Vincent's waist and helped him down the stairs. Verina had moved down to the lowest level and waited for him in the easy chair.
"You look like a little higher grade of shit," she said.
Vincent sat down on the couch. "You don't have to follow Nathan."
Verina gave Steopa a sharp look. He left the room.
"Yes, I do," she said.
"He knows you are a friend of mine."
"Give me a little credit. First, vampires don't have friends. We have potential rivals. And second, he likes women, dead or alive."
"Verina, what are you doing?"
She tossed her hair back. "Stroking his ego mainly. I told him that I wanted to be around a strong vampire. That you were too weak. He believes that."
"It's too risky," Vincent said. "What if he finds you're here?"
Verina smiled. "Whatever Ogden did to the top floor makes this place hard to find. This is the safest place in the city."
Vincent rubbed his neck. The welt was still there. "What have you found out?"
"He thinks the werewolves finished you off." Verina smiled.
Vincent's head snapped up. A smile crossed his face like a twisted snake.
Verina nodded. "Yeah, I know. So he has not even been looking for you. Harry is his vassal and a pervert. He didn't stop his "fun" with Janice, even when she was dead."
"That's sick."
"I know," Verina said. "I know he's the one who uses the drugs." She leaned forward. "He drugs them, then Nathan puts the thrall on them. That's why it's so deep."
"They told you this?" Vincent asked.
"I watched them," Verina said. She sat back, waving her hand in front of her face. "It turned my stomach."
"So there's another woman at his place?" Vincent asked.
Verina nodded.

Vincent punched the wall behind him. “What the hell? If you are going to hunt, you hunt and kill, you don't go half-ass about it. If you want to string the prey along, you don't force them.”

He covered his face with his hands. “What about the ghoul?”

“I don't know,” Verina said. “He won't talk about her.” She recrossed her legs. “There is something else, Ogden sensed it.”

“What?” Vincent asked.

“His books have a thrall on them.”

“How could he do that?”

Verina shrugged. “Ogden is working on it. He thinks it has to do with the words.”

Vincent sat back. “It would explain why his fans are so... fanatical. But Rebecka and Andi did not fall for it, so it must be weak.”

Verina shook her head. Her curly hair covered her face for a moment. “You should know, you have to have the right mindset to be in a thrall.”

“True. I never go after a meal in the 'Keller unless they are attracted to me first.”

“Right. You have to find the right mind to work with; some are too strong.”

“Rebecka could always block me out, even when she was human,” Vincent said. “I would never force any of them. He does, with the drugs.”

“Like a frat boy using a date rape drug.”

“He's a ravisher,” Vincent said.

Rebecka and Steopa came down. Rebecka came over to Vincent, holding out her closed hand. “I want to give you something.”

Vincent held out his left hand. Rebecka opened hers. Laying on her palm was a necklace. A red jewel hung off a simple gold chain. It looked like a ruby, except it had liquid on the inside. The liquid rocked back and forth. She turned her hand and let the necklace drop on to his palm.

“Thanks,” he said.

Verina's eyes went wide. “Rebecka are you sure you want to part with that?”

“It doesn't seem to affect men,” Rebecka said. “Steopa tried it on he didn't feel any different.”

Vincent placed it around his neck. His neck felt warm. He

touched the jewel.

"You neck is healing," Verina said.

Vincent felt his neck. Where the chain touched the welt, the welt had disappeared. He smiled. "Thanks, Rebecka."

Rebecka smiled back. "We're leaving for the night. The computer is up and running, there are books to read. But you should not leave, at least not yet."

Verina nodded. "I agree. You leave this place and Nathan will know you are not dead."

"Sounds like you guys are putting me under house arrest," Vincent tried to joke.

"Think of it as a quarantine," Verina said. She stood up. "I have to go now, too. Nathan will get suspicious if I do not show up."

"Hey, what about Toby? The musician?" Vincent asked.

Verina shrugged. "He wants a living girlfriend now."

Vincent waved at them. "Sure, leave me here all by myself. I'll be fine."

"You are a big baby," Verina said.

"I was almost destroyed," Vincent said.

"You won't be alone. Ogden will be coming by later."

"Okay." Vincent waved them on.

After they had left, Vincent stared at the computer. He had played poker on the one at John and Lorelei's apartment. He had never understood why some people, like Rebecka, would spend hours on one. But there was nothing else to do.

Vincent sat down and turned it on. He brought up the browser. He had to admire Rebecka. This computer sat underground in a cemetery and some how she got high speed Internet hooked up to it.

He typed in *Ashes at Dawn*. The list came up. Vincent cringed. He wondered if any other writer had fans that were fantasizing about the writer more than the novels. These women -- the majority were women -- did love the books, but the conversations all turned to how sexy Nathan Stout was.

Vincent typed in the name Nathan Stout. He read the official biography. He admired Nathan; the page did not give any information away that could be checked. Vincent scanned through a few more links, then found a gem on a gossip blog.

"I had a chance encounter with Nathan Stout. I am not sure if he really believes the stuff he writes or not, but I had the strangest time with him. I don't want to say much, because it was too weird. But his teeth are very sharp."

Vincent giggled. He reread the entry and giggled again. After he composed himself, he looked over the local news site. Nathan was sloppy. The bodies of his previous victims had been found. Janice had been the last one.

"That could have been Andi," Vincent said.

He leaned back in the chair and wondered if that phone call Rebecka had Swen make to his cop friend Grady had anything to do with the bodies being found.

Vincent felt another vampire approaching. He turned in his seat to see Ogden walk in. Ogden smiled. "Good, you are awake."

He took off his hat. "Has anyone told you what has gone on since your attack?"

"Yeah," Vincent said. "Verina said you found something odd in the books."

Ogden nodded. "Yes, I was reading the German translation, and found some differences. When I started to do the comparisons, I realized there were certain words in the English language were causing a thrall. It may explain why his books are constantly trashed by non-English-speaking critics."

"Verina told me the books were called crap in Italy."

"They were nicer than the French," Ogden said. He sat down on the couch. "Where did you get that?" Ogden asked, pointing at the necklace.

"Rebecka gave it to me." Vincent turned off the computer monitor and turned to Ogden. "It helped heal my neck."

"I see."

"Do you know what is going on with the Coiree?" Vincent asked.

Ogden nodded. "That it filled itself with fresh blood as soon as you were brought here? Yes. It seems to want to protect its protectors."

"You sound like it is aware." Vincent said.

"It is." Ogden said. "When you were dragged in here, the cup filled with blood. Steopa had the smart idea of dumping the blood on you. That is what saved you from turning to a corpse when the sun came up.

“Thanks for putting that block up around this place.”

Ogden tilted his head. “I don't follow.”

“When you cast that protection spell...”

Ogden shook his head. “No, that would have just blocked intruders. Whatever is blocking anyone from sensing you are in here, the Coiree is doing it.”

“So if I want to leave, I have to carry that with me.” Vincent scoffed.

Ogden stared at Vincent's necklace. “Perhaps not.” He pulled his gaze away. “I will have to do some more study, but I think there might be a way for you to leave and still be protected from Nathan sensing you.”

He pulled his cane closer and rested his chin on it. “On the subject of Nathan, how are you going to take him down?”

“I haven't thought about it.”

“You should. Were you alive when duels were commonplace?”

“Only the rich would do it,” Vincent said. “The guys I hung out with, we would settle scores with our fists.”

“But you are familiar with the concept?” Ogden asked. “I have an idea. One that will make the playing field even. I have heard, but have never witnessed, a vampire duel called the Blood Duel.”

“What is that?” Vincent asked.

“It is a proper challenge to another vampire. Once it is made, the challenged vampire cannot get out of it, or bring any others into the fight.”

“Interesting. How's it done?”

“It is simple. You just have to issue the challenge and name the place. Then you spill your blood on the ground. Once it is set, all vampires in the area will come and witness it. There will be no way the outcome will be altered.”

“That sounds like a good idea.” Vincent said.

“But you are not ready to fight him yet.” Ogden said. “I know, I used to be a doctor.”

Vincent chuckled.

“So, he has a pet ghoul,” Ogden said. He left the sentence hang in the air like a question.

Vincent nodded. “He called her Angelica.”

“That's interesting, because the love interest in *Ashes at Dawn* was named Angelica. Perhaps his time in India was not the only truthful thing he wrote about."

"That thing might have been his girlfriend?" Vincent asked. "I would have killed her."

"Some people think any sort of existence is better than none. That is why some humans insist on living wills. They don't want their family to keep them in limbo," Ogden said.

"Yeah, but I know what it's like," Vincent said.

"Verina alluded to that as well. I am sure you have a fascinating story." Ogden crossed his legs and did not say a word.

The silence went on. Vincent felt like he had to speak. "You want my story. Here it is. I was killed on the slab under the Rathskeller, as you know. But I didn't die. Joshua somehow trapped me. I could not do anything against him. He kept me hungry. He wanted an assassin to take out rivals. I was good. I could go into a home and wipe out all the family in a matter of seconds. No one would know how they were killed."

Vincent paused. "Decades he kept me like a pet. I don't know what leash he used. Then one night, I get this visitor. It was Verina. She had been invited to his mansion for a little get together to discuss the looming prohibition laws. She found me in the basement."

Vincent paused again. He waited for Ogden to say something, but he didn't. He's better than some psychiatrists, Vincent thought. "She comes back days later with someone else. He was the one who held back Joshua. Joshua did know some magic, but Verina's friend knew more. When Joshua was killed, I was free. That first meal, Joshua's blood. It tasted like shit, but it was the best meal I have ever had."

"Who was her friend?" Ogden asked.

"His name was Thomas," Vincent said. "He used to live around here, but moved down south a few decades ago."

Ogden seemed satisfied. "I knew we had similar stories."

"You were made by a mad magician too?" Vincent asked.

Ogden gave him a small smile. "I was the mad magician, but I had help. My wife had been killed by her own brother, because our marriage made us class and national traitors. She was Hindu, and I was a British officer. Marrying outside your class at that time was social suicide. Your family, friends, and community would have turned against you."

Ogden paused. “I had tried praying. God wasn't listening. So out of desperation I went to a temple of Kali. She heard me. I don't remember actually dying. I do remember coming out of the temple changed. My brother-in-law did not survive the next dawn.”

“You never regretted your decision?” Vincent asked.

“If you had to do things over, would you have wanted to die on that altar?”

“Hell no.”

Ogden smiled. “Same here. I have to go upstairs, do you want to join me?”

Vincent hesitated. “If I can.”

He tried his legs, he stood up without any sway. He followed Ogden back up to the chapel. Vincent felt the necklace get warmer. It was a very pleasant feeling, like an already warm bed on a cold night. Ogden walked over to the Coiree. He glanced at the necklace on Vincent's neck.

“That's interesting,” he said.

Vincent glanced down. The jewel glowed red. He walked up to the Coiree. The blood started to shimmer. The closer Vincent got, the brighter the glow became. Vincent felt the jewel move. He looked down, the jewel pointed toward the Coiree.

Ogden passed his hand over the Coiree. “They are related,” he said.

Vincent touched the Coiree. The warmth from the necklace filled his whole body. A thirst took over Vincent. He picked up the Coiree, and took a long drink. He felt warm all over.

He felt better. The necklace settled back down and laid on his chest. He touched it. It was not as warm as before. The warmth had past from the jewel to his body.

“Do you feel any different?” Ogden asked.

Vincent nodded. “I feel better.”

The blood level in the Coiree rose. Now that Vincent saw it happen, any doubt he had about where the blood had come from was pushed out his mind. There seemed to be so much more going on right now. Vincent did not want to speculate on what was happening. He wanted to concentrate on the matter of taking care of Nathan.

Ogden rubbed his chin. “I have to do some more research on this.”

Vincent patted the necklace. “I will say this: Rebecka has a good eye for finding odd things.”

Ogden did not respond. He walked a few steps to the stairs, then turned around. “Think about what I told you. About the duel.”

“I will,” Vincent said.

Vincent walked Ogden to the entrance. Ogden replaced his hat, then said his goodbyes. When Ogden had gone, Vincent sat down on the couch. He did not like the idea of Verina pretending to enjoy Nathan's company. But she was good at that. He wanted to hurt Nathan now, but in such a way that Nathan would be confused. Something to throw him way off the scent of anyone close to Vincent.

There was one way to do it. Vincent smiled to himself. Time to bring in his hidden ace. Time to get Swen involved. Vincent stopped himself from laughing out loud when he thought that. He doubted Nathan realized what Swen was. If he had any clue, Nathan probably thought Swen was a werewolf. Vincent giggled. Would Nathan even understand that Swen was a berserk? If he didn't, Vincent grinned to himself, what a wake up call.

CHAPTER 11

Vincent didn't like the quiet. He sat down on the couch and forced himself to sigh. He had stayed in Forest Grove before. Lorelei had found him in the small chapel at the top of the hill almost a couple of decades ago. That had been a black time in his existence. But his stay now felt like a prison sentence. He had been here for a week. It felt like months.

He went over to the computer, tapping his fingers against the monitor. He checked on the Burgundy Rathskeller's website, then on the one for Third Eye Curios. Thursday meant DJ night. John would be running the booth. He looked around the old smuggler's store room. It felt small, cold, and alien.

Vincent found the Deerbow City's Historical society site. He clicked through the pictures, remembering how the city looked when he was alive. Before he was killed, he had a pretty good life for a human. He had been working his butt off trying to save enough money to move out to California. It was too late for working in the gold mines, but he had his eye on the coast and working the piers.

His life wasn't a party, but it wasn't a waste either. But since Verina saved him, he had more fun now. Part of it was the knowledge that the things that held him back before -- the lack of money, the illnesses, the grind of working, and being from the wrong side of the tracks -- meant nothing to a vampire.

Vampires were more concerned about how you affected them. If you were going to be a threat, or someone they could tolerate. There were some that would pretend that your status before mattered. But that would not save them in a fight.

He had money now, thanks to liberating all of Joshua's wealth. The man had never believed in banks. Verina had found the vault. They spent a lot of it the first year he was free. It had been the roaring Twenties; money bought you friends.

Vincent found a picture of a New Year's Eve ball. He stared at the photo for a long time. In the background stood Verina and him. In the photo, it was not too clear where they were, but Vincent remembered that night. After the balloon drop, they had taken another couple out for a walk.

He felt Steopa and Rebecka approach. He shut the computer off and hurried to the couch. He felt his face, had he been crying? What the hell? he thought.

Steopa ducked into the room first. "Teodor is sure," he said to Rebecka as she came into the room.

"If you say so," Rebecka said.

"I did not, he did."

"Hi, guys," Vincent said.

"You look better," Steopa said, removing his hat. The snow from his hat hit the floor, spreading over the stones.

"I feel better," Vincent said. "What's been going on?"

"Nothing much," Rebecka said. "Teodor and his boys have been reporting on Nathan."

"Except for Chuck," Steopa said. "He will not leave Andi."

"It's sweet."
"He is protecting her," Steopa said.
"That's good," Vincent said. "So Nathan is still around?"
"Yeah," Rebecka said. "He was on the TV before we came over here."
"Ogden came by yesterday. He suggested a Blood Duel."
Steopa smiled and nodded. "That would be a good idea."
"You know of it?"
"I have done it. Nathan will have to face you."
"What if he takes off?"
"He will not be able to." Steopa rubbed his chin. "Where do you want the fight?"
"I hadn't thought about that."
"This would be a good place," Steopa said. "Away from human eyes, and all the vampires in the city can find it."
"Yeah, it would be a good place. Wait a minute, all the vampires in the city?"
Steopa nodded.
"How many would that be?"
Steopa shrugged.
"You know what I was thinking, getting Swen to scare Nathan, before I challenge him."
"You mean you want Swen to go after Nathan?" Rebecka asked.
"No, just put some muscle to him."
"Why?"
"Because I don't want Nathan to rest easy. I want him to be on edge. You get on edge, you make mistakes. Perfect time for someone to come back from the grave," Vincent said, then added, "again."
"But to put Swen in danger... I see. If Nathan does anything, Swen gives him a bear hug."
"And you can't charm a berserk," Vincent said. "I know, I've tried."
"If Swen agrees," Steopa said.
"Yeah, that's the problem. I can't make him."
Rebecka scoffed. "Just ask him. Swen will."
"Ogden doesn't think it is a good idea for me to leave yet. Swen would have to come here." Vincent looked at the door. "If there was a way to shield me from Nathan."

"Tin foil hat?" Rebecka asked.

Vincent scoffed.

"Do you want me to call Swen?" she asked.

Vincent nodded.

Rebecka went back outside.

"You should spend your time now figuring out how you will defeat him," Steopa said.

"Easy, I kill him," Vincent said.

Steopa didn't smile. "There are many ways to approach a battle. Brute strength works. But the best way is to make your opponent make mistakes that you use to your advantage."

Vincent thought. "He likes tricks. He did this vanishing act that was impressive."

Steopa raised an eyebrow.

"He totally disappeared," Vincent said. "He was still there, but I could only sense him when he lost concentration. He was not in the shadows, it was like he was invisible."

"I have never seen that."

Vincent shrugged, "Neither have I. Until Nathan."

"What about his vassal?" Steopa asked.

"I could just kill him," Vincent said.

"You could, but once the duel is set in motion, you can only harm each other at the intended place and time. You cannot harm the others that are under the protection of your opponent."

"So he can't touch the Rathskeller and I can't harm Harry?"

Steopa nodded.

"So what do you suggest?"

"I saw you get inside that skinhead. If you could do the same with Nathan?"

"Yeah, if he gives me an opening, because there are two ways I will not take."

Steopa looked at Vincent for a moment with a blank face, then he laughed. Vincent stepped back. He had never heard Steopa laugh before. It was like your pet cat asking you to pass the milk one morning.

Rebecka's voice echoed down the old smuggler tunnel. "Hey guys, come here."

Steopa stopped Vincent from leaving. He touched the side of his head. Vincent sighed. I hate being stuck here, he thought.

He stood in the doorway and tried to look around Steopa. Steopa pointed up the stairs. "What is she doing here?" he asked.

"I tried to stop her," Rebecka said.

Vincent sniffed. He could smell the perfume that Andi liked to wear. Oh no, he thought.

Steopa looked over his shoulder, then moved to the side. Andi looked down at the top of the tunnel. She pushed by Rebecka and Steopa and ran to Vincent.

"Oh my god! I shouldn't have made you go," she said. Tears welled up in her eyes. "You and Chuck were right."

"Whoa," Vincent said. He smiled at her and rubbed her shoulders. Andi wiped the tears from her eyes.

"I'm so sorry," she said.

"How did you find me?"

"Chuck told me. I thought you were dead for good this time."

Vincent glanced up at Steopa. His face had gone dark. He shook his head. Vincent almost brought Andi back into the memorial, but he stopped. What if Nathan was still in her head? He thought.

"I don't think it was a good idea to come here," Vincent said.

Andi looked up at him with hurt eyes. "But it's my fault."

"I would have gone, eventually."

Steopa loomed behind Andi. "This is dangerous."

Andi jumped when he spoke.

"He's right," Vincent said. "We are sure Nathan thinks I was destroyed. But now that you are here, he might find me again."

"I'm so sorry. I'll go," she said.

Steopa stepped aside. Vincent tried to stop her. Steopa growled. She ran back up the tunnel and past Rebecka, who was talking on her phone.

"That was stupid of her," Steopa said.

"Just leave it, okay?" he snapped at Steopa, then he growled. Steopa raised an eyebrow, but said nothing.

"You don't have to make it any worse," Vincent said.

Andi screamed.

Vincent ran up the tunnel and outside. Rebecka stood ahead of him. She paused at the small pyramid. Vincent stopped when he saw why Andi screamed. A ghoul scrambled after Andi. She ran back toward Vincent and Rebecka.

The ghoul scuttled on the ground like a crab. It reached out with its claws. Andi tripped. She jumped up before Vincent reached her. She landed four kicks on the ghoul's head. It backed away to try for another attack.

Vincent got between Andi and the ghoul. The ghoul hissed at him. This ghoul had been a large man in life. Now the flesh hung off him like a large suit on a stick. The folds of the skin gathered around its arms and legs. The folds of extra skin made the ghoul's neck disappear.

It jumped. Vincent blocked the attack and threw it off him. The ghoul opened its mouth wide, like a hungry snake. It tried to scuttle around the other side of Andi. Vincent jumped and kicked it.

The ghoul growled with a moaning, rasping noise. It jumped sideways, landing on a gravestone. Vincent shoved Andi toward Rebecka and Steopa. She tripped over a tombstone in the snow, cursing. The ghoul jumped. Steopa swatted it with a sword he pulled out from underneath his long coat. Andi crawled behind Rebecka.

Vincent hissed. The ghoul screeched. The noise rang in Vincent's ears. The folds of its skin shook. It leaped and knocked Vincent to the ground. He wrapped his hand around the ghoul's neck. The folds of skin covered Vincent's hand in a pile of decaying flesh.

It screamed.

Vincent felt his necklace heat up. The heat traveled through his body and down to his hand. The skin surrounding his hand began to char and turn black. The ghoul screamed.

Its mouth opened wide enough to take Vincent's head off. It tried to pull away. The screaming continued as Vincent's hand heated up. The ghoul's skin smoked. It yanked away from him. Vincent slapped his other hand on the ghoul's head.

Where he gripped its head, a black charcoal outline of his hand print appeared. Underneath his palm the ghoul's flesh turned black, then smoldered red. It clawed at his arms, but Vincent roared and forced the ghoul down to its knees.

He wanted to see this ghoul go up in flames. Vincent chanted, "Burn, burn, burn."

His necklace glowed, bathing the ghoul in a red light. The red light accented its gruesome features. Vincent's hands felt hotter. The skin on the ghoul went from ash charcoal to red and yellow flames. Smoke rose up from its body, making Vincent shut down his sense of smell.

"Gross," Andi said behind Rebecka.

The flesh on the ghoul blistered, popped and ignited. The burn started on its head and moved downward. Vincent could only feel the heat on his hands. The flames from the ghoul touched his flesh, but he did not burn. Vincent held on. The ghoul stopped screaming. It burned into a pile of ash shaped like a ghoul.

He removed his hands. The ash blew over the snow, leaving a gray smear on the cemetery. The snow had melted where the ghoul burned, but none of the heat had harmed Vincent. He turned around.

Rebecka's ring had a slight glow to it. She stared at his necklace. Vincent touched the jewel; there was no heat.

"How did you do that?" Rebecka asked.

Vincent picked up a handful of white snow and cleaned his hands off. "I think I like that necklace you gave me."

Steopa closed his eyes for a moment. "There is something else."

"What?" Vincent asked, brushing the ash off his clothes.

"I cannot sense you," Steopa said.

Rebecka paused, she cocked her head to one side. "He's right."

Vincent grinned, an evil, happy grin. "Really?"

Both Steopa and Rebecka nodded.

Vincent laughed. "Good. Nathan won't know what hit him."

"Do you still need Swen?" Rebecka asked.

Vincent nodded. "Oh yeah."

Andi gripped Vincent's arm. "What was that?"

"A ghoul," Vincent said.

"Those are supposed to eat corpses, right?"

"Well, the ground is hard. And all the meat is frozen, so you would have been a treat," he said. "Like cherry pie."

Andi hit his back. "Jerk!"

Vincent laughed again. "It's true."

"You can be a bastard!"

"Hey, you were the one that came to a cemetery at night and alone," Vincent said.

She hit him again. "Still a bastard."

Vincent giggled. Then he cleared off a stone slab and sat down on it. "I think it's time to rethink my attack on Nathan. I got the magic hands now."

“If Nathan will let you get close enough,” Steopa said.

“What?” Andi asked. “You are going to fight Nathan? After he almost killed you?”

“His pet ghoul almost killed me. I can't wait to put that bitch out of her misery,” Vincent said.

“Why don't you let it go?” Andi asked.

Vincent turned to face her. She stepped back, her eyes wide.

“Because he screwed with my friends, he tried to kill me, and he is an asshole. That's why! I should have never allowed him into the Rathskeller!”

He kicked over a statue of a civil war solider. “I let him in because I thought he could control himself. He tricked me! No one does that to me twice!”

“Vincent, I-” Andi said, hiding behind Rebecka.

He turned to face her, knowing his glamor had dropped. Andi screamed into Rebecka's shoulder.

“Andi, this is now between him and me. I want you to stay out of it!”

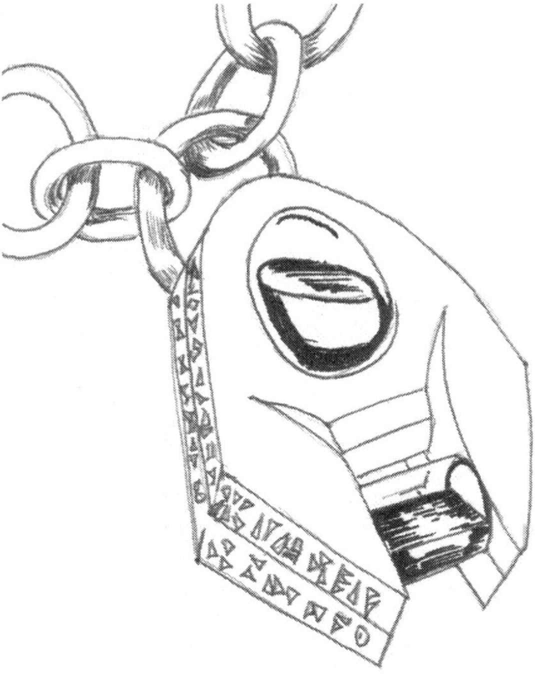

CHAPTER 12

Vincent had another week to recover and to think. Swen had agreed to put a little terror into Nathan. He should have been planning his attack on Nathan, but Vincent began to think of the old days.

The smuggler's tunnel had been a familiar haunt of Vincent's. Staying in the old cellar made him remember a lot of the old times. Running bootleg alcohol, because Verina and him were bored. Waiting in a public restroom for his victim to come in and stopping their heart before they had realized he was there.

He had been going out into the graveyard at night and practicing so he could become like he had been. A killer.

Every night since he had killed the ghoul that attacked Andi, Vincent hunted the other ghouls in the cemetery. How humans never noticed how many of these creatures there were, he never knew. Forest Grove had its own congregation of ghouls.

Vincent found that most ghouls buried themselves close to the columbarium. He had wondered if the smell of cremated remains attracted them. Vincent would hurry out of the mausoleum as soon as the sun set and wait for them to dig themselves out.

The ground would look undisturbed, then the ghouls would push themselves out of the earth. Small mounds would dot the area around the columbarium. The mounds would break apart to reveal a ghoul emerging.

There were at least fifteen at Forest Grove. It was hard to imagine that there had been that many vampires in Deerbow. But then Vincent didn't know much about ghouls. Could they make more? Did they live as long as vampires? He didn't want to find out either.

Tonight, Vincent waited until the stringy, red-haired female ghoul shambled pass him. He had watched her the night before. She still looked human; her transformation from vampire to ghoul must have been recent.

She sniffed the air like a bear. Then she lowered her head and crawled over the snow, stopping at each grave. Vincent walked on top of the snow, staying a few feet behind her.

The ghoul stopped at a grave and dived into the snow. A cloud of white billowed up behind her. Vincent watched her dig into the hard ground. Soon dirt flew out of the grave. Vincent walked up to the edge of the hole. The ghoul smashed her fist into the top of the coffin.

"Hey, beautiful," Vincent said.

The ghoul snapped her head up. She narrowed her eyes, focusing on him and bared her teeth.

"Food ain't too good tonight, is it?"

She sunk into the grave, tensing her muscles.

Vincent blew her a kiss. "Come on, sweetie, let me take you out of your misery."

She jumped out of the grave, aiming for Vincent. He turned into a mist and appeared on the other side of the grave. The ghoul spun around. Vincent smiled.

"Ah, did I get away from you?"

She threw herself across the open grave. Vincent wrapped his arms around her as she finished the arch of the jump. He threw her against the gravestone. The ghoul twisted her body around just as she was about to hit the stone. She crouched on it like a decaying gargoyle.

Vincent opened his hands. The necklace glowed bright. He glanced at his hands; they turned red. The ghoul screamed. Vincent roared. He blurred and slammed his hands down on her body. He burned her face.

As she screamed, he turned to a mist and disappeared into her open mouth. The ghoul choked. Smoke came out of her mouth and her nose. She clawed at her chest. Her nails dug a long furrow into her breast. The flesh under the cut blackened, then glowed red. She exploded.

Vincent solidified, shook the ash off his coat and returned to the Dysart Memorial. Ogden stood outside the entrance. He raised his hand in greeting as Vincent approached.

"Interesting hobby you have taken on," he said.

Vincent laughed.

"Do you intend to kill them all?" Ogden asked.

"I am just trying to get in practice again, that's all."

"Practice?" Ogden tapped his cane against the angel statue. "I see, you think you are no longer a killer?"

"I didn't like the drop that Nathan got on me." Vincent shoved the statue. The entrance to the tunnel slid open.

"Forgive me for asking, but did you ever hunt other vampires?"

Vincent shrugged. "A couple," he said. "But only if they deserved it."

"Nathan does?"

"Come on, you know he does."

They went back into the memorial. Ogden removed his hat and gloves. "Can I play devil's advocate for a moment?"

"Yeah, sure."

"What Nathan has done is impressive. Casting a thrall with words. A thrall so powerful that he not only had rabid fans of his writing, that some look upon him as a sex symbol. Lord Bryon would be jealous."

"You like him now?"

"No, he is still rude and arrogant. But some vampire might admire his powers. I for one have been trying to figure out how he does it."

Vincent studied Ogden's face. He looked older, as if he had been not sleeping, but that would be impossible. "What is it?" Vincent asked.

"I don't think this is a vampire thrall." Ogden reached into his coat pocket. "I found this."

He handed Vincent a slim volume of poetry. Vincent opened it. The pages were old and falling out of the binding. It had been printed a long time ago, Vincent recognized the style of typeface. But behind the printed words were other words, in a faded brownish color.

"What is this?" Vincent asked.

"This book was given as a gift to a royal from an admirer. It caused quite a scandal at the time. She ran off with him, leaving a marriage of ten years. It was strange because this was the only correspondence they ever had before she left."

Ogden pointed to the faded words. "You see those words. They were written with a mild acid onto the paper. The paper was then printed with the poetry. The words behind the poetry are what caused her to leave."

Vincent closed the book. "You said you thought he did something with the words? Is this it?"

Ogden nodded. "But it's not a vampire thrall. It's a spell. Anula searched the novel on the computer. You know what she found, the same spell, worked into the writing. Only this time he did not hide it in the paper. It was written in with the prose."

"You're kidding me?"

Ogden shook his head. "I would be careful, because I found the first mention of the spell. It is in a book that has a binding spell for a vampire."

"What?"

"A spell to keep a vampire as a pet, so to speak."

Vincent's hand shook. "Are you sure?"

Ogden nodded.

"Could that spell, for instance, make the vampire do whatever you say?"

"It is a very strong thrall. I was almost affected myself, but

Anula brought me back."

Vincent growled. "You know this spell?"

"I do."

Vincent shook his head. "For years I could not figure out how Joshua kept me prisoner. This must have been it, or something similar. Bastard never fed me. Those kills I made for him were the only time I drank blood."

"You must have been starving," Ogden said. "But you did not become a ghoul?"

"I never did. I came close, but I never had the urge to eat human flesh."

"It could be the same spell. But-"

"You got your car?"

"Yes, but-"

"Let's go for a ride."

Vincent pulled Ogden out of the memorial. They went to his car, with a quizzical look from Manas. Vincent told him the address. Ogden shook his head.

"I do not think that it would be a good idea to take this car into that neighborhood," Ogden said.

"Why not? They are going to think you are a drug dealer."

"Very droll."

Before Manas pulled the car away from the curb, he reached into the glove box and took out a handgun. He drove the car to Joshua's old house and pulled up to the house. Vincent got out. Ogden leaned back into the car and gave some instructions to Manas. He drove off as soon as Ogden turned around.

"What do you think?" Vincent asked

"Colonial?" Ogden asked. "In this part of town?"

Vincent grinned. "I will give you the grand tour."

"There are people inside."

"It's out of the cold. What do you expect?"

They went to the back of the house. The back door had been nailed shut. Vincent ran his claws down the door, then he hit the door with his fist. The door cracked and splintered. He kicked the door. It fell into the house.

Ogden wrinkled his nose. "Obviously the plumbing does not work."

"I don't think these squatters would care if it did," Vincent said.

"Charming."

A gaunt young man peered around the corner. Ogden raised his cane. The young man ran deeper into the house. He yelled for someone named Cormac.

Vincent walked in. "Honey, I'm home!"

A baseball bat swung out toward Vincent. He knocked it away, like an annoying bug. A tall man glanced at his now empty hands. Vincent pointed at him.

"You Cormac?" he asked.

The man did not respond. Ogden walked passed Cormac. "Can you show me what you wanted to show me? I do not like... slumming."

Vincent grinned and dropped his glamor. Cormac pressed himself against the wall, his chest pounding up and down.

Ogden gave Cormac a little nod and walked deeper into the house. Vincent pointed. "It's in the basement."

"You can't goes there," Cormac said.

Vincent spun around, he lifted Cormac up. "You cannot tell me what to do. This used to be my home, asshole."

He threw Cormac into the nearest wall. Someone on the other side of the hole made by Cormac's body screamed. Vincent went over to the hole and peeked in.

"Hey! It's Kitcat," he laughed.

Ogden tapped his cane. "Vincent."

"Fine, I'll show you the basement."

He led Ogden down to the coal bin. Ogden walked around the outside of it for a few moments. He tapped his cane against the ornate metal work. "This should not have held you," he said.

"It did."

"For how long?"

Vincent shrugged. "Thirty years."

"Hmm." Ogden ran his finger along the metalwork. "There is silver in this and a few other metals. Interesting alloy mix." He peered into the metal lattice. "Ash. This was a vampire cage."

"So it could have been the metal and the wood?" Vincent asked.

"I doubt it. Look at this place. It has been stripped of anything valuable. But they left the metal here. It repels them as well."

Ogden ran a hand along his cane. His lips were moving, but Vincent could not make out what he was saying. Then he hit the coal bin with his cane. The metal melted. The black and silver liquid ran together in a large puddle on the floor. Ogden reached out with his gloved hand to the wall.

"Ash, with writing," he said. "Yes, this is the same spell."

"Step away," Vincent said.

Ogden stood back. Vincent stared at his hands until they glowed yellow. He slammed his palms against the ash. He felt the searing pain of the wood for a moment, then the heat from his hands burned the ash. He stepped back and watched the fire spread from two palm prints, up the wall.

"The whole house will go up," Ogden said.

"Let the damn thing burn." Vincent turned to go back up the stairs.

Ogden placed his hand on Vincent's shoulder. The basement disappeared. When he could make out the world around him again, he sat in the back of Ogden's car.

"Now we know about the spell," Ogden said.

Vincent nodded after the weird sensation of nausea passed.

"And we know that Nathan changed it to affect humans."

Vincent didn't answer. He watched the city pass by.

"How did you escape?"

"I told you. Verina," Vincent said. "She saved me."

"Why did you change?"

"What do you mean?"

"When you are at the Rathskeller, you are the host, you serve drinks. You are the life of the party, if you will. But, you weren't then. What happened?" Ogden asked.

"I was sick of living in crypts."

"So you adjusted and changed so you could be around humans, without causing fear. Commendable." Ogden motioned to the city. "But there are some out there that deserve to die, don't you agree?"

"I can think of one."

"You tamed your beast. But I think the beast needs to come out again," Ogden said. "The trick is knowing when. Nathan is good with words. That is his power."

"Then I rip his vocal cords out."

Ogden smiled. "Do the Blood Duel and you can. When you are ready."

"Soon."

"Good."

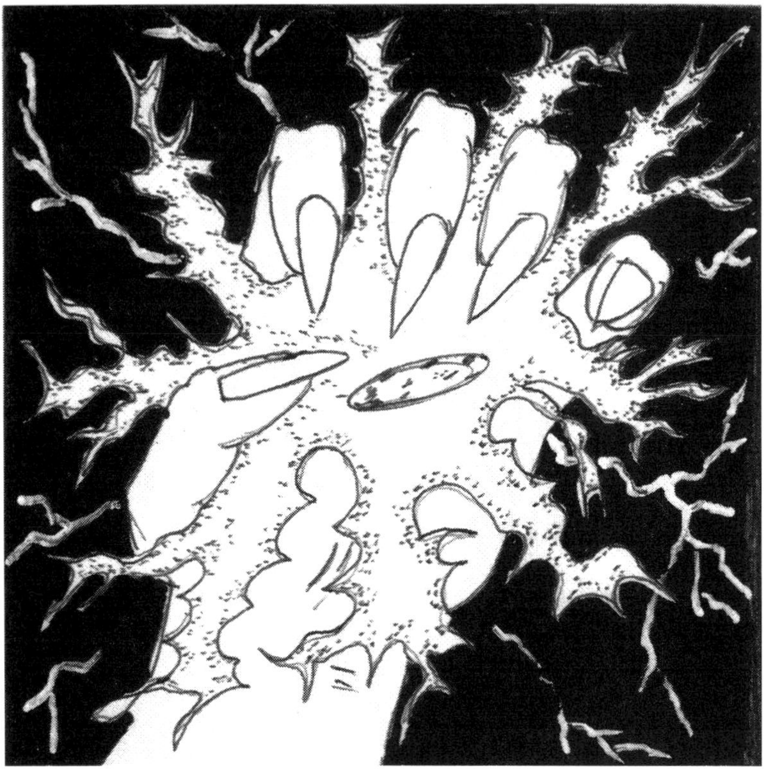

CHAPTER 13

Lorelei juggled the glasses she almost dropped when Vincent appeared in the bar.

"Christ!" she said.

"How's things?" Vincent asked.

Lorelei laid the glasses down on the bar, then pointed to the top balcony. "I should sue that film company. They left drill holes all over the walls up there."

"How much money do you need to repair it?"

"It's not the money..." Lorelei leaned on the bar. "What about you? I heard you got to be someone's dinner."

"Funny. I feel better now," Vincent said. "I'm just stopping by tonight to tie up some loose ends."

"Have you had anything to drink?"

Vincent nodded. "Yeah. Is Swen going to be around?"

"He's coming in late tonight. Cassie and him had an appointment somewhere."

Vincent glanced around the now empty club. "How's business?"

"Good, better, now that creep has stopped hanging out around here."

"Which creep?"

"Which? Mr. Stout?" Lorelei uncorked a wine bottle and poured herself a glass. "He had the guts to show up here, but he was with your friend, Verina. So Swen let him in. She kept him in line, but I still didn't like him being here."

Vincent almost told Lorelei that Nathan had wanted to make her a meal too, but stopped himself. "That was the only time?"

Lorelei shook her head. "He'd show up, sit over at your usual table and had a group of girls around him. He doesn't leave with any of them from here, but shit, we can't kick him out for nothing."

The back door to the bar opened. John came in, placing some take-out bags on the bar. He reached over and shook Vincent's hand.

"Great to see you. You coming back?" John asked.

"Not yet. I shouldn't be here now, but I hate that crypt."

John unpacked the take-out dinner. "How much longer?"

"I got things to do before I come back," Vincent said. He sat down at the bar.

Lorelei turned to John. "Are we still going out with Andi and Chuck?"

John nodded, his mouth full of a sandwich.

"Where are you all going?" Vincent asked.

"There's a concert on Monday we want to see," Lorelei said.

"If the weather holds," John said.

Lorelei's cell phone rang. She grabbed her sandwich and phone. Turning her back, she walked to the other side of the bar.

"What do you think of Chuck?" Vincent asked.

John shrugged. "He's a good kid. That night you went after Nathan he got his brothers and father down here in a hurry."

Lorelei came back. "Damn, Swen can't make it in."

"What happened?" John asked.

"They got the results back. Cassie can't have kids."
John's shoulders sagged. "That sucks."
Vincent stared at Lorelei for a moment. "Wait, they were trying to have kids?"
"For about a year now," Lorelei said. "Cassie could hardly speak on the phone."
"That's too bad," Vincent said.
Lorelei sighed. "I'm glad we don't want any. I would hate to go through that."
John caught Vincent's eye. Vincent got them impression John didn't fully agree with Lorelei.
John sat down next to him. "So what is going on?"
"I wanted to talk to Swen about something, that's all," Vincent said.
Chuck came through the back door. He grabbed a glass off the back of the bar and poured himself a soda. Lorelei informed him about Swen not coming in.
"I can watch the booth," Chuck said. He pointed at Vincent. "Andi told me what happened at the cemetery, thanks."
"She shouldn't have come out," Vincent said.
"Have you ever tried to stop her?" Chuck shook his head. "She's tiny, but she can hit."
Lorelei glanced at her watch. "You gonna stick around awhile?" she asked Vincent.
"I could."
"Why don't you go get some of the kegs from the basement?"
"What are they doing there?" Vincent asked.
"We had to move them for the movie."
"I'll go with you," Chuck said.
Lorelei sighed. "Chuck, that basement is-"
"Weird?" Chuck asked. "I can smell it up here."
Vincent spun on the barstool to get a better look at Chuck. Was he joking, he thought. "What can you smell?"
"Blood, mainly," Chuck said. "It's got me curious."
Vincent slid off the stool. "Okay, but if you start growling, I'm pulling you out."
Lorelei handed Vincent the keys. Chuck followed him outside to the basement entrance.
"Wouldn't have been easier to make a doorway into the

Rathskeller?" Chuck asked, as Vincent unlocked the door.

"We tried. Lorelei kept getting sick," Vincent said.

Chuck gave him a strange look.

"She's a bit psychic."

"Oh."

Vincent opened the door and turned on the lights. The main room below the stairs was the electrical room. Vincent could see the kegs sitting in the room next to that one.

Chuck followed Vincent down. When he made it to the bottom of the stairs he stopped as if he had hit a wall.

"You okay?" Vincent asked.

"Yeah, just give me a minute," Chuck said. He turned his face away. "There's a lot of blood."

"It was a slaughter house."

"Then why do I smell human blood?"

"The owners didn't fire all their bad employees," Vincent said.

Chuck grimaced. Vincent noticed his teeth had grown longer. "You knew about this, and you still bought the building?" Chuck asked.

"It's why I bought the building," Vincent said. "Anyone else would have tried to make this part of the building workable. That would have been a mistake."

Chuck nodded. "I see. Like what happened to that developer a few years back."

"What do you mean?"

"At Jacob's Landing. You know how it butts up to Greenwoods? I just started college, and this guy was buying up all the land. The students were protesting it," Chuck said.

"Yeah, I remember."

"Well, do you know why he backed off suddenly? The rumor is he found the old village and saw something there that freaked him out."

"The old workers village? When I was alive, that was a nice place."

"You can't find it now," Chuck said. "I found it once. It was weird. I had this wolf trailing me the whole time. I can talk to them. I mean, well..."

Vincent waited for Chuck to find his words.

"But this wolf watched me the whole time. It looked like it was grinning. I tried speaking to it. It shook its head and head butted me until I left. Weirdest thing ever to happen to me."

"It head butted you?"

"It was pushing me out of there."

"That is weird." Vincent picked up a keg. "You're not pulling my leg are you?"

Chuck picked up the next one, with both hands. "Nope, I went back with my brother. We thought maybe a new werewolf was in town. We could not find that village."

Vincent picked up another keg. "I would check it out, but I don't know the vampire out there."

"Why do you need to do that?"

"Because it's proper," Vincent said. "I go in there without introducing myself, instant fight."

Chuck waddled with his keg as they went back to the stairs. "The only werewolves in town are my family."

"Must be nice."

"Until you want to settle down with a mate. Pickings are pretty slim."

"What about Andi?"

"I can date humans," Chuck said. "She's the first who figured it out."

Vincent sat one of the kegs down so he could open the door. "Andi had Swen figured out on the first night they met."

Chuck put his keg down and breathed deeply. "She's smart and a sweetheart."

Vincent felt Nathan nearby. He opened the door to the back room and shoved the kegs in. He handed the keys to Chuck. "Nathan," he said.

Chuck growled. "If he comes here-"

"No!" Vincent patted Chuck on the shoulder. "Don't do anything to him, unless he makes the first move. And do not tell him about me."

"Like I would talk to him."

"He might mess with your head again." Vincent felt Nathan approaching. "I'm heading up. Tell Lorelei, sorry."

"All right, all right," Chuck said, dragging one of the kegs away.

Vincent scrambled up the side of the building to the top of the Rathskeller. He jumped to the next building and stood in the shadow of the large billboard.

He only could sense Nathan. Verina wasn't with him. Vincent scanned the street. He saw Harry first. He drove a car into the nearest parking garage. Vincent leaped from the billboard to the top of the parking garage. He turned to a mist.

Harry parked the car on the floor below. Vincent drifted in with the snow and slight wind. Harry got out of the car. Nathan opened his door. Vincent would have groaned if he was in his solid form.

Nathan had dressed in the latest fashion for men, but had added his own touches. The silver skull necklace glinted against his chest. His top hat had a black silk ribbon wrapped around it and hung down his back. Around the rim, he had attached rose stems.

"Can we make this quick?" Harry asked. "She's been acting out lately."

"Don't worry. I secured the door. She won't get out," Nathan said. "We both learned our lesson in Chicago."

"That vampire didn't fill her up. We need a good meal this time."

"I know." Nathan grinned. "I have people meeting us there. It will be easy tonight."

Vincent drifted behind them as they left the parking garage. Just as they were about to walk onto the street, Nathan turned as if he heard something. Vincent slid underneath a nearby car.

"What is it?" Harry asked.

"I thought I felt something..." Nathan said. He shook his head. "I must be hungry."

They did not head to the Rathskeller. Vincent followed them to a smaller club a few blocks away. Vincent slid in the door as they entered. The smell of many different blends of coffee filled the air.

Nathan and Harry took a seat in the middle of the room. The table sat in front of the door, making it the first table you saw when you walked in. A small stage sat to the front with a single chair on it.

There were no waitresses. Harry went over to a counter and ordered their drinks. The menu had only coffee and teas, no wine. How is he going to play the hurt poet now? Vincent thought.

Two women walked in, one much older than the other one. The younger one pointed to Nathan and nudged her friend. Vincent realized that they had similar facial features. Mother and daughter? he thought.

Nathan stood up. “You must be Marisa and Joyce.”

He bowed. The women giggled, the younger one blushing from her neck to her cheeks.

Vincent drifted along the back booths. He floated up the wall and hung in the shadows. He had a great view of Nathan's table.

“Marisa,” Nathan said as he pulled out a chair.

The younger woman sat down. Nathan pulled another chair out for Joyce. She sat down as Harry came back to the table. He sat down the coffee and smiled at Joyce.

“Would you two like anything?” Harry asked.

Joyce shook her head.

“I'm glad you came,” Nathan said.

Vincent watched him charm the two women. They had a small conversation about his writing, during which Harry watched Joyce. Vincent risked exposing himself and touched Harry's mind. He only saw one image, but it was enough to make him pull back.

He touched the minds of the two women. They were both in Nathan's thrall. Vincent tried to read their minds. He felt Nathan pushing his way in. He pulled back before Nathan could feel him.

Harry moved his chair closer to Joyce. She smiled at him. A young man walked up onto the stage.

“Good evening everyone, we are going to have a good time tonight...”

Vincent floated around to a darker spot near the bar. A solo musician came up to the stage and sat down on the chair. The sound of an acoustic guitar filled the room.

A while later, Joyce excused herself. Vincent drifted behind her. He slid into the bathroom as she shut the door. The bathroom had only one stall. Vincent waited around the ceiling.

Joyce came out of the stall. She had a dark shroud around her. Vincent could not believe his luck. She walked to the sink, washed her hands, then dug into her purse for her makeup. Vincent slid down the wall and solidified behind her. He did not bring up his glamor.

She applied her lipstick. In the mirror, Vincent looked like a shadow behind her. He leaned close to her ear, his chin almost resting on her shoulder. Joyce's hand froze in mid-apply. Vincent growled in her ear.

“You like vampires?” Vincent asked. He whispered the words,

but the question echoed in the bathroom.

Joyce's mouth opened. She drew in a breath. Vincent misted and entered her body. He choked the scream that had been building. He shoved her back. Vincent had control of her body in a few seconds.

He lifted the lipstick and finished applying it to Joyce's lips. Vincent did not feel her fight back, but he did sense Nathan touching her mind. He put a small block up. He hoped it would look like she had been drinking.

Vincent threw the lipstick in the bag. He took a few steps and stopped. He walked like a man. A few moments of rearranging of some neurons, and Vincent tried again. He swung her hips, like she had when she left the table.

He forced Joyce to walk back to the table. She started to fight back. Vincent slammed her down. He sat down at the table, grabbing Harry's drink.

"Sorry, I guess I am thirsty," Vincent said. He did not have to force her body to work for him as much as he had in the bathroom. It was like riding a bicycle: once you learned, you never forgot.

He downed the rest of Harry's coffee. It burned the inside of Joyce's mouth, but Vincent did not feel the pain. He knew her body had; the synapses went crazy.

"I could get you whatever you like," Harry said.

"Sounds good, toots."

Harry left the table. Marisa stared at her mother. Vincent pinched Marisa's arm. "Live a little, sweety."

Nathan laughed.

Marisa leaned over and whispered in Joyce's ear. "Mom what's wrong with you?"

"It's the music."

Harry returned with the coffees. Vincent winked at him. Harry sat down. Vincent took over Joyce's sense of smell. He could smell a drug in the coffee. He pulled away from that sense when he felt Joyce push back. He downed the second coffee just like the first. This one burned the back of her throat.

"Tell you what," Vincent said. He felt Joyce back off. "Why don't you and I get another table and let these two have a private conversation."

Marisa grabbed Joyce's arm. "Mom, you promised."

Vincent sensed it. A bit of fear surfaced in Marisa's mind. He shook off her grip.

"It will only be for a few minutes."

"Mom?"

Nathan patted Marisa's hand. "It's all right."

Vincent felt the thrust of Nathan's mind into Marisa's. Her eyes clouded over; she moved her chair closer to Nathan. Harry glanced at Nathan while he stood up.

"We'll be fine," Nathan said.

Vincent shoved the chair back before Harry had a chance to pretend to be a gentleman. Joyce's chair hit Harry in the stomach. He pulled his hands back, with his face turning red. Vincent couldn't tell if it was anger or embarrassment. Vincent made Joyce laugh.

"I guess I don't expect a man to be a gentleman," Vincent said.

"It's fine," Harry said. His voice had an angry edge.

They left the club. Vincent glanced down the street at the Rathskeller. There wasn't a line, but the people hurried into the doors. Harry walked with Joyce down the street toward the parking garage.

"How long have you known Nathan?" Vincent asked. He made Joyce grab Harry's arm.

"Over a decade now," Harry said.

"It must be weird to be a famous writer and have women fawning over you?"

"They don't fawn over me."

The further they moved away from Nathan, the more Vincent could enter Harry's mind. Vincent shivered, not from the cold, but from what he saw in Harry's head. The images of blood and violence were swishing around his mind. Two emotions hit Vincent: disgust and arousal.

I am walking with a wannabe serial killer, Vincent thought.

Vincent felt the drugs that had been put in Joyce's cup starting to take hold of Joyce's body. She stopped fighting Vincent and disappeared. Vincent smiled.

He touched his head. "Oh, I don't feel too well," he said.

"Maybe it was too much coffee?"

Vincent saw two people walking toward them. He turned to Harry, wrapping his arms around Harry's shoulders.

"I know what you did," Vincent said.

"What?"
"I know what is in your condo."
"What the hell are you talking about?"
"Who was she? Someone you screwed after Nathan had his meal?"
Harry tried to step back. Vincent held on to his shoulders with an iron grip. "You can tell me."
"How do you know-"
Vincent wrapped around Joyce's heart. He squeezed. Then he snapped some of the nerves at the base of her brain. Her last breath left her body in a rasping noise. Vincent left with it. Her body shook, then crumbled. She hit the ground, dead.
Harry jumped back. He looked around. The people that had been walking toward them ran to Joyce.
"Is she all right?" one of them asked.
"Ah, we were just talking," Harry said. "She just fell."
"She's not breathing."
Vincent let the wind take him back to the Rathskeller. He solidified on the roof and leaned on the wall. A small crowd had gathered around Harry and Joyce. Not the best kill, not even a needed kill, Vincent thought. But she served her purpose.

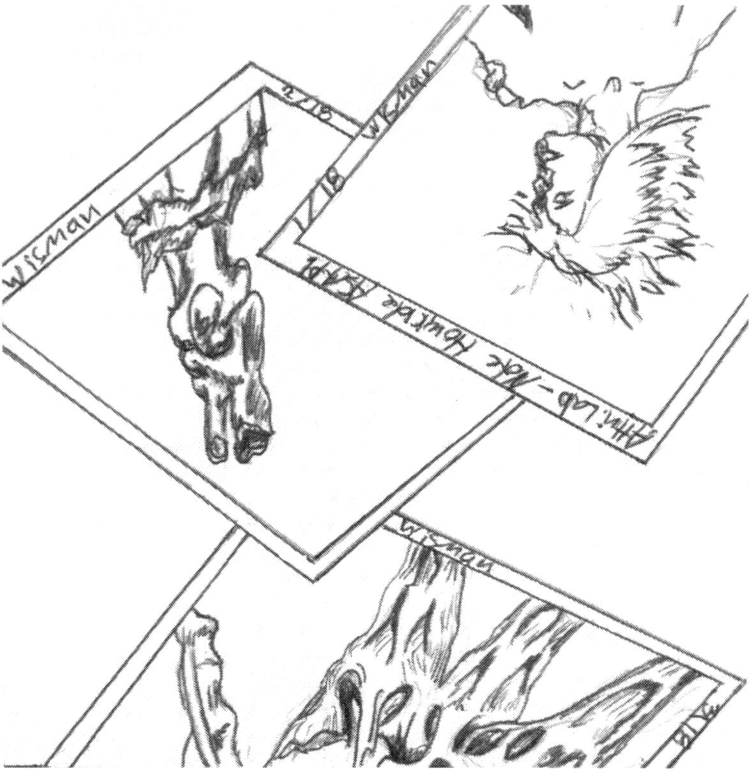

CHAPTER 14

It was time.

Vincent waited along the street that ran outside Forest Grove. He could feel another oppressive snowstorm moving in. He could smell the snow in the air and feel the weight of the clouds as they gathered. The wind became stronger in the short time Vincent stood on the sidewalk. Vincent trained his ear to the road.

He heard the rumble of Swen's winter rat of a vehicle. The old beat-up pickup truck that Swen had said if he ever crashed it, you wouldn't be able to see the new dents. It ran well. It ran in the coldest weather. The main thing was, it ran.

The truck pulled up and idled. Vincent got in. Swen had bundled up. He wore a fur hat and thick mittens, with a hole for the index finger to be exposed. He still had on his leather jacket, but he had thrown a heavy parka on over it. He looked like a Viking heading out to chop wood in the back forty. Vincent tried not to laugh.

Swen turned to Vincent and shrugged. “Damn heater went out,” he said, his breath accented by the white mist formed with each word. “Got just enough heat to keep the windows clear. But I don't think you will notice.”

“I'm fine,” Vincent said. “So what's been going on?”

Swen put the truck in gear, it sputtered and complained, but he got it to move. “Well, that Harry showed up last night. That took a lot of balls. He wanted to take a look around. I kicked him out. He wasn't wearing anything to dress code anyway.”

He turned a corner. “Andi feels like shit. She thinks she got you in a lot of trouble. I told her that fights like this are so common with vampires, that they should take numbers.”

The truck fish-tailed. Swen swore at it, and got it back on the road. “So I am making sure everyone is extra safe. Chuck and Andi are moved into Rebecka's old place. Cassie wishes I would sleep at home, but hell, she knows I wouldn't be able to.”

“Cassie's a great lady,” Vincent said.

“Yeah she is. Not many women can put up with berserks. It takes a lot of patience.” Swen smiled.

“So where have you been sleeping?” Vincent asked.

“In Cassie's back room at Third Eye Curios,” Swen said. “She doesn't mind unless I snore.”

Swen moved the truck onto one of the main thoroughfares. The plows had been out, but the roads were filling up with snow. The smile disappeared from Swen's face. “So what do you want me to do this guy?”

“I want to make him jumpy,” Vincent said. “Then I will move in with the challenge.”

“I don't do this for anyone,” Swen said. “You or Rebecka, fine, but no one else.”

“What about Steopa?”

Swen scoffed. “I don't think he would ever need my help.”

“We should find Verina, she will know where Nathan is.”

“No need to.” Swen reached over and tapped on an envelope on the dash.

Vincent took it. Verina's handwriting covered the envelope. He opened it and read the note inside.

"Dear Vincent,

"Nathan is still not aware that you survived. I have heard your idea. I think it is foolish, but you always seem to have the luck of a fool.

"I will suggest we go to a club downtown, Brickhouse, around eleven PM.

"Yours always,

"Verina."

Vincent folded up the letter. "Brickhouse?"

Swen sighed. "Brickhouse. That's that rich kids' playground."

"I see."

"But across the street is Hog Heaven," Swen said. "I know the guys there."

"What the hell is a biker bar doing downtown?" Vincent asked

"Do you know how much a new bike costs? It's hard to be poor and a biker nowadays. Oh, these guys are good guys. Some of them even go out to rallies. But they like to drink close to their jobs."

"Oh, so this is a biker bar with Armani leather?" Vincent asked.

Swen laughed. "You could say that."

He looked out the windshield and up. Swen sighed. "That storm is getting bad. We better get there before it opens up."

"Swen, you can say no."

Swen grinned. "Let's see, this puffed up romance writer comes to the club, screws with our friends, tries to kill you, and you think I would say no."

The falling snow made a hypnotic pattern against the windshield. Vincent scraped some of the frost off on the inside. "I heard that you and Cassie want kids."

"Yeah."

"I thought you told me it would be a bad idea."

Swen sighed. "That was when I was just hired, remember? I still had my buzz cut. I didn't want kids then. But the last few years Cassie and I talked about it. Finally agreed and look what happens."

"Sorry man."

"End of my family line," Swen said. "I think I am the last

berserk."

Swen put the truck in a lower gear and they turned onto the exit for the downtown. He parked his truck in a parking garage not far from either place. Swen left his outer coat and his hat in the cab of the truck. As they walked to the stairs, Swen coughed.

"Grady is gonna meet us there," Swen said.

Vincent stopped. "You read the note."

"Sorry man, but Grady is watching Nathan too," Swen said.

"So the cops are onto him?"

Swen nodded. "Yeah, but they can't link him directly, you see."

"You trust Grady?"

"Come on man, what type of question is that? Ever since Kuwait, I wouldn't trust anyone else."

They walked up to the door of Hog Heaven. Vincent glanced across the street. Brickhouse looked like a neon whore. In the snowfall, the neon blurred and faded like a watercolor painting. Vincent reached out with his mind. Verina had not arrived yet.

Swen opened the door to Hog Heaven. Vincent had expected a rough and tumble type of place, the type of place where blood was spilled on a nightly basis. This was not it.

It still looked like a biker bar. Pictures of motorcycles filled half of the walls; the other half were filled with pictures of nearly naked models. Some of the patrons were in leather. Vincent noticed that Swen was the only one who wore his colors.

The food that the waitresses were serving was typical bar fare. Burgers, sandwiches, fried vegetables, and lots of it. There were a couple of patrons eating salads, but these were large, topped with meat and cheese. You had to look close to even see the lettuce.

Swen walked to the back of the bar. Vincent followed. Some of the patrons glanced up at Vincent, but as soon as they saw he was with Swen, they went back to their conversations. At the back sat a black man. Swen sat down opposite of him.

"Hey Grady. This is Vincent," Swen said.

Grady nodded. He had a shaved head and looked as if he was as tall as Swen, but with a lighter frame. Grady's frame was made for running. Vincent could see him playing the fullback position in football.

He stuck out his hand. "How ya doing?"

Vincent took his hand, aware that Grady would feel the coldness of his skin. Grady didn't seem to care. Vincent noticed for a second his eyes flickered like he was expecting something else. Vincent sat down.

"He was in Mr. Stout's apartment," Swen said, pointing to Vincent with his thumb.

"You saw Janice Wisman?" Grady asked.

Vincent sat back and waved his hand. "Wait, is this an official interview?"

Grady shook his head. "You will remain anonymous. If I was to put in my reports that I got my information from a vampire or a berserk, I would be locked up."

Vincent glanced over at Swen. Swen gave him a slight nod.

"I did see her. She was near death the first time. When I went back, she was dead," Vincent said.

"How long?" Grady asked.

"The way she smelled, a few hours, tops."

Grady ran his hand over his bald head. "That just confirms what we know."

Swen tried to get the attention of one of the waitresses. She held up one finger to tell him it would be a little bit. Swen sighed.

"Vampires don't eat human flesh," Grady said. Even though it was stated, it still sounded like a question.

Vincent shook his head. "We could, but like humans, we find it distasteful."

"Most humans. There are the few sickos. A large part of her arm was missing, along with a thigh."

"That would have been the ghoul," Vincent said.

"What is that?"

"A ghoul was a vampire, but one who, because of bad choices or lack of opportunity, did not drink blood."

The waitress chose that moment to appear at the table. She gave Vincent a strange look. He smiled at her with his charming smile. She blushed. The waitress took Swen and Grady's order, looking at Vincent oddly again when he didn't order anything. When she had gone, Vincent leaned in and continued.

"It has to be human blood. You know that saying, you are what you eat? Well, vampires are what they drink. The more animals you drink from, the more you become like an animal. Until one night, you are a ghoul. You are always hungry. Only this time, blood ain't gonna do it for you. You have to eat flesh. They aren't too picky about where it comes from."

Grady nodded. "I think I've seen one, before I joined the Marines and got my life back on track. I was running with some bad kids. I was being chased one night, so I cut through Chapel Hill's cemetery. This guy came out of nowhere, almost attacked me. I was already running full speed so he missed me. But it wasn't until hours later I remembered how the guy moved. Close to the ground, but fast."

"A friend of ours says they remind her of badgers."

"Yeah, that's it."

The waitress came back with the beers. Grady had ordered a shot chaser. After she left, Grady downed the shot and continued. "So how does this ghoul fit in?"

"Nathan keeps it like a pet," Vincent said. "He drinks his victims, draining them over a period of days, and when they are dead, feeds them to his ghoul."

Swen put his mug of beer down. "Why the hell would he want to keep something like that?"

Vincent shrugged. He had wondered the same thing. He felt the approach of Verina and Nathan.

He nudged Swen. "We have to go."

Swen downed the rest of the beer. "Sorry, brother."

"It's all right, man," Grady said.

On their way out of the bar, Swen stopped to give the waitress a large tip. Vincent glanced over to the TVs. The bartender had turned one of them to a weather report. This storm wasn't going to blow over in a few hours. They were expecting it to last at least two days.

This will not be a night to be out late. Tomorrow would be a night to stay home and stay warm. You would have to be a fool, or someone with an appointment to keep, to go out in it. Vincent smiled to himself. Tomorrow night he will have Nathan to deal with. It wouldn't matter what the weather was like. Vincent would have a good time.

But all that hinged on what was about to happen. Vincent glanced at Swen. Swen had a dark look on his face, as if he was mentally preparing to go to battle. Swen nodded. They braced themselves and went outside.

The wind hit them like a sheet of ice. The snow came down harder in heavy, large flakes. Swen pulled the collar up on his leather jacket. Vincent's hair whipped into his face. The blowing snow gave them a small curtain of privacy.

Across the street, a limousine pulled up to the Brickhouse. Nathan got out and held open the door for Verina. Vincent nodded to Swen. Swen cracked his knuckles and walked into the street. He didn't have to worry about traffic. The storm had made the streets almost clear.

Vincent watched, stepping back into a space between Hog Heaven and the next building. He faded into the shadows. Verina glanced in his direction and smiled at Swen's approach. Swen walked up to Nathan. He stood a foot taller than Nathan. He reached over and poked Nathan in the back. Nathan turned around. Vincent concentrated and got to hear Swen at his finest.

"What do you want?" Nathan asked.

"What the fuck did you do to Vincent!?" Swen shouted over the wind.

"I didn't do anything to him," Nathan said. "Excuse me, it is very cold."

"Like you could feel that, blood sucker." Swen struck his palm against Nathan's shoulder.

"Who the hell are you?" Nathan asked, all pleasantness gone from his voice.

"The bouncer at Vincent's club," Verina said. She tried to light a cigarette, but the wind blew out her lighter.

Nathan grinned. "Missing your employer?"

Swen grabbed Nathan's shirt collar and picked him up. Vincent saw the surprised look on Nathan's face.

"You shouldn't have done that," Nathan hissed.

For an answer, Swen threw him. Nathan flew into a nearby alley. It wasn't just Swen's strength that sent Nathan into the alley. Nathan had changed direction in mid throw; otherwise he would have hit the wall of the Brickhouse.

Steam rose off Swen. He removed his jacket and bellowed. Verina's eyes went wide in surprise. She stepped aside as Swen stampeded into the alley. Vincent jumped over the street and on top of the Brickhouse. He looked down.

The snow blew across the mouth of the alleyway. Inside the

alley, the ground was still bare. Nathan stood up as Swen entered the alley.

Swen had gotten hairier. His nose began to elongate, along with his jaw. He pointed at Nathan, his hands turning into large paws with human-like digits.

"Bastard!" Swen roared. "Cowardly, slimy, leech! Blood sucking tick on my ass! I'm going to rip you apart!"

Nathan hissed and dropped his glamor. He looked like a pale, sickly clerk. The vampire life-styler look was nothing like his real vampire face. Nathan slashed at Swen's chest.

Swen grabbed Nathan's hand and squeezed. Each bone broke in turn. Vincent could hear the bones break from the roof of the Brickhouse. Nathan growled. Swen roared. Verina walked into the alley. She took her time, watching the events in front of her with a bored look. With no wind in the alley, she took out her cigarettes and lighter.

"Fight him!" Nathan yelled.

Verina blinked. Vincent felt that mind blast. Verina made a show of lighting her cigarette. "He doesn't have a problem with me," she said, blowing the smoke out.

Good girl, Vincent thought. She stood at the entrance of the alley, her one arm crossed in front of her chest, her other elbow resting on it. She smoked the cigarette while watching Swen threaten Nathan. She glanced up at Vincent. Her fingernails had grown longer.

Swen picked Nathan up by his broken hand and smashed Nathan against the wall. Swen bellowed. The snow melted and turned into steam as soon as it hit Swen's skin. Even with the cold, Swen lost his human form.

Vincent jumped down, landing behind Nathan, and tapped Nathan on his back. Nathan spun around. His eyes grew wide when he saw Vincent. Vincent smiled. "Hello, Nathan."

"How?" Nathan screamed.

Swen lunged forward. Vincent held up his hand. "Swen, back off!"

Nathan shook his head. "You should be dead!"

He never took his eyes off Nathan and he said, "You should really make sure someone is dead before you assume they are."

Vincent grabbed Nathan and shoved him against the wall. "This is gonna end, you bastard!" Vincent hissed. "I am calling you out. I am going to make sure you turn to ash when the sun rises."

"You don't have the guts."

Vincent growled "You don't know what I can do. We will end this tomorrow."

"Why not now?"

"We are doing this by the book. Yeah, vampires do have rules, which you are ignoring. So here it is. Tomorrow at midnight, Forest Grove. We will finish it."

Vincent let go of Nathan, then he cut his wrist with his thumb. The blood dripped on to the ground. "Will you meet me there?" he asked.

Nathan sneered. "I don't have to."

Swen growled. Verina walked over. Her high heeled boots clicked on the cold blacktop. "You better," she said, smoke drifting past her face. "I will make sure all the other vampires know you refused to fight Vincent. You will not be able to go to any town, village, or city on this world without them knowing you are a coward."

Nathan looked at Verina, then at Swen, and finally focused on Vincent. "I'll do it," he said, his voice full of vile.

"I'll see you tomorrow. Just you and me, and there will be witnesses." Vincent flicked some of his blood on Nathan's face.

Swen snorted. Vincent nodded to Swen. "Go cool off, buddy," he said.

Swen went to the street. Vincent watched over Nathan's shoulder. Swen sat down in the deeper snow, then rolled in it. Vincent hid his amusement.

Nathan spun on his heels and shook his finger in Verina's face. "You traitorous whore!"

Verina looked at him, with a cool, calm, icy stare. She blew smoke in his face. "I'll see you tomorrow, Vincent."

She turned and walked out of the alley, stepping over Swen at the entrance. Vincent smiled and nodded. "I will see you tomorrow"

As he walked past Nathan, Nathan tried to strike Vincent. Instead of hitting Vincent, he cried out in pain.

Vincent shook his head. "Idiot, you will only hurt yourself until tomorrow. Don't you know anything?"

Vincent kept his poker face on as he walked out of the alley. Swen sat next to the building, shirtless, the snow melting around him. The snow that hit his skin turned to water and ran down his chest. Vincent reached down and helped him up.

"Okay, Swen. Lean on me, we can't have Nathan see you like this," Vincent whispered.

Swen nodded. He stood up, holding his jacket and shirt in his hand. Swen walked away from the alley. When they had finally entered the parking garage, Swen sagged.

"Can you drive?" Swen asked.

Vincent shook his head.

"Let me cool off first," he said.

Swen leaned against the cold concrete. His shoulders started to shake. It took a moment for Vincent to realize that Swen was laughing. Swen raised his head. "That was actually fun."

Vincent patted Swen on the back. "Maybe you should come by tomorrow?"

Swen shook his head. "No, I think I will still be recovering. We lucked out. Thank the gods for the temperature drop."

Vincent nodded. They were lucky that Swen hadn't lost it. Having a full berserk running around in a snowstorm would not have been a good idea. Vincent sat down next to Swen. He rested his head on the cinder block. He reached up and touched his necklace. It was warm. Tomorrow he would use it in the fight with Nathan. He never told Nathan the Blood Duel had to be a fair fight.

CHAPTER 15

Vincent drank from the Coiree. The bricked-up windows of the upper chapel did not allow any view of the snow that the storm had left, but Vincent could feel that the snow had buried most of the memorial. He could not feel any other vampires around. Odd, he thought. He always felt one or two in the back of his mind. He put the Coiree down.

He closed his eyes and cleared his mind. How had he killed before? Nothing could stop him. Somewhere deep inside, he had put that killer asleep. He just had to wake it up again.

A redness filled his closed-lidded eyes. He opened them. The Coiree glowed, filling the small chapel filled with a soft red light.

The blood in the cup became very still, a mirror surface.

Vincent could see his reflection. He had not seen his face clearly reflected in anything for a long time. His face had not changed. His hair, goatee and mustache had been fashionable when he was alive. He still looked as young as he remembered, but his eyes looked ancient.

He stood over the Coiree studying his face. Then he felt another presence in the room. Vincent raised his head and looked around. In the space where the cross would have been stood a shadowy figure. Its wings spread over the back of the chapel. It stepped out of the shadows and lowered its wings.

"You have my gift."

Vincent recognized the voice. It was the one that had spoken to him when his throat had been cut and in the dream he had after Nathan had tried to destroy him.

"You again," Vincent said. "It wasn't a dream?"

The figure shook his head. "I find it easier to speak to you in your subconscious. You are fighting soon?"

Vincent nodded.

"You must kill him."

The figure leaned forward, a shadow reaching out to Vincent. "Vampire Altus must survive. That one, the one that tried to destroy you, is a Vulgaris."

"I thought we were just vampires?" Vincent asked.

"No, there are two different bloodlines. Both of you can claim to be real vampires, but only one bloodline is not tainted."

"What do you mean?"

"An Altus will not fear my blood. A Vulgaris will burn."

Vincent looked over his shoulder at the Coiree. Behind him the figure said. "Yes, it was hidden for you."

"Yours?"

"No, but it was made for the Altus. Only they can use its powers." The winged shadow bowed. "I made sure it was hidden."

"Then I owe you my thanks," Vincent said. "One question. What are you?"

"You will not understand yet."

"Fine. Can I have your name?"

"Not yet."

Vincent felt it disappear like a ray of moonlight traveling across his body. He could handle strange things, but something about this winged visitor did not scare him as much as chill him. If its appearance was to reassure him, it did not.

He went to the lower level and sat on the couch. There was nothing to do but wait. He willed himself to shut down for a short time. When he felt the first vampire approach, Vincent stood up and dropped his glamor.

Vincent walked up the old smuggler's tunnel. At the tunnel's entrance, the weight of the snow felt more oppressive. Vincent started to push against the door, but then thought better of it.

There would be other vampires in the cemetery. Many he had only felt and never had met. He had no idea what the ambitions of these vampires were. They might not feel him inside the memorial, but once he left they could find it. Ogden had made it clear that he was one of the protectors of the Coiree. After it had saved him, this place had to remain hidden.

He misted. Traveling under the door through the snow, Vincent reappeared by the angel statue. No wonder the snow felt oppressive underground: at least four more feet had been dropped on the already deep drifts. The cemetery looked like a sea of white, with man-made islands breaking through the top of the snow. The smaller stones were completely covered, some were only shapes under the snow. The entire place looked like a watercolor study in black, white and gray.

The snow had stopped falling. Vincent could tell that the plows had not passed by the cemetery. Humans would not be fully dug out of this mess for at least a day. But this would not stop any of the vampires.

Vincent wondered how many would show. He never knew how many were in the city because he learned early on that you do not broadcast yourself to other vampires you did not know. Some liked to take out the competition.

Those days were fun, Vincent remembered. Verina had left him on his own; she had wanted to see Italy again. And Vincent, being stupid, had sought out the other vampires. Most wanted him out of their territories, others wanted him dead. He won every battle, but then he had been made for killing. The times had changed.

He felt the first vampire come closer. Vincent had never seen her. She reminded Vincent of his teacher at the one-room schoolhouse he had attended. She wore her hair in a tight bun and a sensible long coat. She glanced at Vincent. He could tell by the look in her eyes she knew why she was here, and that he was not a threat to her now.

A tall, elegant black vampire appeared near the pyramid. She had high cheek bones, and wore an African-style scarf on her head. She carried herself with a regal walk. Vincent could feel that she was old, but he had never sensed her until now. She did not look at him.

Verina came next, wearing a black dress. That's not a good sign, Vincent thought. Then Verina caught his eye and smiled. She came up to him.

"I still say you're a fool," she said.

"Maybe."

"None of us can help."

"I know."

"But I do know you can do more than kill him."

Vincent watched a young vampire couple come down the small hill. "What do you mean?"

"Destroy him." Verina kissed Vincent on the cheek, then walked over to the rose window side of the Dysart Memorial.

The vampire couple both had a look of confusion on their faces. Vincent could see the collar bones and the sunken cheeks of the female vampire. The young-looking male vampire did not look as if he saw his twentieth birthday. Both of them had the gaunt look of vampires that had not drunk enough human blood.

Steopa and Rebecka appeared behind Vincent, walking arm in arm. The school-teacher vampire stared at them with a sneer of disgust as they came closer. They stood nearest to Vincent. Steopa opened his long, heavy, woolen military overcoat, showing him a long curved sword.

Rebecka glanced over at Vincent. She moved toward him. Steopa stopped her. He said something to her in what sounded like Russian. Rebecka gave Vincent a sorry look. She said something to Steopa in the same language, but she spoke it with hesitant pauses, biting her lip while she thought of a word to say.

Ogden approached with another vampire that Vincent had never seen. The unknown vampire and Ogden were in a whispered conversation as they found a place to stand. The stranger had his dark hair pulled back into a short ponytail. Both of them dressed as if they were going to head to the opera after the duel.

A male vampire jumped down from the trees. Tall and slender with short hair, he looked like he should be writing code. But there was something else, a crazed look in his eyes, the way his body tensed; he reminded Vincent of a time bomb about to go off. He glanced at all the vampires in the circle, smirking.

A heavyset young-looking vampire with a buzz cut walked by Vincent and straight over to Steopa. He slapped Steopa on the back and laughed. Steopa turned around and shook the younger vampire's hand.

"Jeremiah, it has been too long," Steopa said.

"How are you, big guy?" Jeremiah asked. He hugged Steopa with one arm.

"Fine, fine. This is Rebecka."

Jeremiah shook Rebecka's hand. "Has he told you about me?"

"No," Rebecka said.

"We will talk after..." Steopa said. He motioned to Vincent.

Vincent closed his mouth and shook his head.

Jeremiah had been followed by a Native American. He stood as tall as Vincent, but more muscular. He glanced around the circle before his eyes settled on Vincent. He nodded. Vincent did not know if that was approval, or just an acknowledgment.

"Fine, Steopa, you just don't want to tell her about how great I am," Jeremiah said.

Steopa laughed. The school-teacher looking vampire jumped. Verina caught Vincent's eye and giggled. The circle of vampires quieted down.

They waited for Nathan. When he came into the circle, the school-teacher's mouth dropped open and she almost said something, but then clamped her mouth shut. The young woman elbowed her companion in the ribs.

"I told you it wasn't an act," she said.

Nathan sneered. Vincent touched his shirt to make sure the necklace laid flat, then walked to the middle of the circle. Nathan walked up to Vincent. He had dropped his glamor as well.

"Do you really want to do this?" Nathan asked. By the tone of his voice, Vincent could not tell if Nathan was issuing a threat or pleading with him to stop.

"You know I do," Vincent said. "You have outstayed your welcome. You tried to destroy me. And you fucked with my friends, people under my territory, and in my cache." Vincent smiled. This one wasn't charming. This one meant he would go for Nathan's throat.

Nathan swiped his claws across Vincent's chest. He misted before the claws hit him. He solidified behind Nathan and swiped at him. Vincent made contact. He sliced through Nathan's back, making three deep gashes. Nathan arched his back and cried out.

Nathan spun around, but Vincent misted behind him again. Vincent grabbed Nathan by the head and ripped into Nathan's neck with his teeth. Nathan buried his claws in Vincent's shoulder. The pain shot through him like a gunshot. It burned like acid had been dropped into his wounds.

Vincent misted, leaving Nathan standing on the snow, holding his hand out. He looked like he was trying to pick an apple that wasn't there. The pain spread through Vincent's unsubstantial body.

He solidified and tackled Nathan. The snow billowed around them as Nathan sunk into the fresh powder. Vincent raised his fists and pummeled Nathan. He aimed each blow at Nathan's face, trying to destroy that little smirk that still hung on Nathan's lips.

Vincent roared as he connected with Nathan's face. His blood splattered across the white ground, adding the only color to the bleak landscape. He felt Nathan shoot a blast into his mind. Vincent brought both of his fists down and smashed Nathan's nose and cheeks.

Searing pain spread across Vincent's chest. He pulled his fists back. Then pain whipped him in the face. Vincent covered his face with one hand. He saw a glimmer of silver on Nathan's fingers. The bastard had come armed with silver.

Silver did not burn and hurt like ash, but it hurt more than any other metal. The silver tips were on the outside of Nathan's gloves. With his free hand Vincent blocked another strike from Nathan and twisted his arm, breaking Nathan's wrist.

Nathan screamed.

Vincent twisted Nathan's broken hand around. He forced Nathan's silver tipped fingers into his own chest. Vincent slid the glove off Nathan's hand. The silver tips stayed in Nathan's chest. Vincent slammed Nathan's other hand against a gravestone.

Nathan's face healed. It had turned from a bloody mass of broken bones and pulverized flesh to a mass of yellow-tinged black and blue bruises.

"You're jealous," he said, spitting out a tooth as he spoke. "You're jealous, because they came to me in droves. I had to drive them away."

"Jealous? I never had to use drugs or spells," Vincent said. "And I let them go home."

"Because you are a coward. You can't kill."

Vincent raised his hand, now a claw. "Wrong."

He sliced open Nathan's chest. Before the wounds had time to heal, he misted and entered Nathan's body. Entering a vampire body was a little different than taking over a human body. There were differences. The digestion system and circulatory system were nothing like a human's. But the nerves and the muscles were the same.

Vincent found the ones that controlled Nathan's arms and hands. He moved one tendon one way, then pinched a nerve. An impulse went up Nathan's spinal cord. He left Nathan's body through his nose.

Nathan rolled over in the snow, his other silver-tipped clawed hand buried in his stomach. Vincent solidified and kicked Nathan over. Even with the soft cushion of snow, his claws dug deeper into his own body. Vincent dropped one knee on Nathan's back and grabbed his hair. Pulling Nathan's head back, Vincent hissed. "Want to end it now?"

Vincent dragged his claws across Nathan's neck. Blood poured on the ground. Nathan rolled, knocking Vincent off him. He staggered up, clutching his neck. Blood escaped from between his fingers as the flow slowed down.

He kicked Vincent. Knocking Vincent's head, then the rest of his body, backward. Vincent landed hard on a snow-covered tombstone beneath him. His ribs cracked. Vincent gasped, then laid still.

Nathan ran forward. He leaped in the air, twisting his body so he would come down on Vincent with his elbows. Vincent waited until the last second, then misted. Nathan came down on the tombstone, his elbows sounding like kindling being broken as he hit the stone.

Vincent solidified. He felt the necklace burn. The snow around him the snow gave off a red glow. Nathan stood up and staggered. One of his arms hung along his side, twisted.

"We are not different!" Nathan lunged toward Vincent.

The heat from the necklace passed into Vincent's hands. He held both of them up. They glowed red, then flamed. He shook his head. "Oh, we are very different."

He jumped, aiming both of his clawed hands into Nathan's chest. His claws dug deep. Vincent forced his fingertips through the muscles and around the sternum. His claws brushed Nathan's heart.

"Got your heart," Vincent hissed.

Nathan grunted and pulled back. Vincent tightened his grip.

"Let me give you an anatomy lesson," Vincent said, pulling Nathan closer. "I've been in vampire bodies. We are not like humans. The blood is absorbed into our body as we drink. So why do we still have a heart?"

Nathan made a noise. Vincent dug the tip of his claws into Nathan's heart.

"A little blood is always kept there, just enough to help us get through the day, in case we are injured. But what happens if you don't have enough? Hmm?"

Nathan scratched Vincent's face. Vincent laughed. He could feel the blood in Nathan's heart heat up. He pulled Nathan closer.

"Can you feel that?" Vincent asked. "That is your blood starting to boil. I burn that away, even if you defeat me, you won't survive the day."

Nathan screamed, his chest charred black from within. Vincent smelled the flesh burn. Nathan opened his mouth to scream; smoke curled out from between his lips. Vincent pulled his hands out of Nathan's body and grasped both sides of his head.

"Burn, motherfucker!"

Nathan's head caught fire. The flames spread over the rest of his body. Vincent did not let go until a gust of wind blew most of the ash that had been Nathan's head away.

Vincent stepped back. He felt lightheaded, as if he had been drinking. The remains of Nathan's body spread over the cemetery. Vincent leaned against one of the statues and smiled.

Rebecka smiled back. Steopa raised his eyebrow, then nodded. Jeremiah laughed.

"Burn, motherfucker!" Jeremiah said. "That was awesome."

The Native American walked over to the ashes and gathered a handful. Then he let the ashes fall through his fingers. He nodded to Vincent, and turned to shadow. Vincent tried to sense where he had gone, but he could not.

"That was messy," Ogden said.

Vincent dusted his clothes off. "But someone had to do it."

"I will speak with you tomorrow," the dark-haired vampire said to Ogden, then he held his hand out to Vincent. "That was good, yes."

Vincent noted the slight German accent. He shook the vampire's hand. The dark-haired vampire bowed and walked away. Ogden patted Vincent on the shoulder.

"That necklace is special," Ogden said. "I would make sure that does not fall into the wrong hands."

A whirlwind of snow blew up around him. When it had settled down, he was gone.

The skinny male who had jumped down from the trees, stared at Vincent's hands. "That was a neat trick," he said.

He walked away, pausing to let the school-teacher hurry past him. Vincent smirked.

The young couple hurried away. The tall black female walked over the top of the hill. She paused long enough to look Vincent in the eye. He gave her a small bow in return. She raised the corners of her mouth in a smile. Then she wasn't there.

Steopa and Rebecka came over to Vincent. Rebecka gave him a hug.

"I was worried," she said.

"I told her not to be. If Nathan won, I was ready for him," Steopa said.

"Thanks, that's encouraging," Vincent said.

They walked away with Jeremiah. He saluted Vincent as he passed by. That left Verina.

She came up to Vincent, standing there a few moments before a smile broke across her lips. "So, those women at the club who think you are hot are right."

Vincent touched his necklace. It felt cool to the touch. "That's only part of it," he said.

"What about his vassal?" she asked.

"Harry? What about him?" Vincent asked.

"Are you going to kill him as well?"

"I don't know. With Nathan gone, he's pretty much up shit creek."

Verina lit a cigarette. "Except he could find you and get revenge."

"Or he could run."

Verina shook her head. "No, he has the ghoul to take care of. When I was with Nathan, it was Harry who took care of the ghoul."

"How long can he stay? Nathan supported him."

Verina shrugged. "Whatever you are going to do, do it quick."

Vincent glanced up the slope. Steopa and Rebecka were still in the cemetery.

Rebecka. He thought. *I need you two to help me.*

CHAPTER 16

Verina hooked her arm in Vincent's and they walked into the condo building without hitting a barrier or being stopped by security. Rebecka and Steopa stayed outside, watching the exits in case Harry ran with the ghoul.

They crossed the foyer to the set of private elevators. Verina stretched her long fingers out, then used the tip of her fingernail to press the button for the elevator. It left a small indention on the button.

When they got inside, Vincent turned to her. “It would have been quicker to travel through the ventilation shaft.”

“I know, but that ghoul and Harry can't leave that way,” Verina said as she cleaned under her fingernails. “Besides, I want to make sure they leave evidence.”

“Why?”

“I don't think it was fair the way he killed them.” She shrugged. “If it had been just him, fine. But to hand them off to that human and then a ghoul. It was like passing around a joint.”

Verina spread out her fingers. Her nails had grown twice as long and turned grayish black. “Like we should talk.”

“I might play with my food, but only if they are going to live,” Vincent said. “If I want them dead-”

“I remember.” Verina grinned. “What about Harry?”

“I have to hear his excuse first.”

The elevator stopped. Vincent turned to shadow as they walked to Nathan's condo. Verina pulled a key card out of her blouse. She slid it into the slot by the door. The door clicked open.

Inside Harry had his back to them. Vincent glanced at the large windows. His reflection could not be seen, only Verina's. But you had to look to see hers. Her reflection looked like smoke. Vincent misted and slid along the floor.

“Hello, Harry,” Verina said.

Harry jumped. His cell phone hit the floor, breaking apart. Its battery skidded under the couch. “Verina? Um, Nathan's not here.”

“I know.” Verina walked closer to Harry. “I just saw him die.”

Harry took a step back. “Then why are you-?”

“Where's the ghoul?”

Harry walked backward to a table. Vincent drifted along the floor until he was behind Harry.

“Look, Verina, I don't have anything to do with this,” Harry said.

“Bullshit,” Verina said.

Vincent solidified. “What she said.”

Harry shook his head. “I won't let you touch her.”

“You sick bastard,” Vincent said.

The ghoul thudded against the door. Verina glanced in its direction. Harry brought his hand over and slammed it against Verina. She screamed. He dived under Vincent's arms. A thin stake stuck out of Verina's shoulder.

The skin around the stake blistered and burned. Verina wrapped her fingers around it and screamed again. Vincent grabbed the stake and burned it with his grasp. Verina blew the ash away, her skin already starting to heal underneath. Vincent spun around.

Harry had opened the door to the ghoul's room. The ghoul stood in the doorway, she held onto the frame with her ragged claws. She sniffed the air, then flicked her tongue like a snake. Harry threw a heavy blanket around the ghoul.

"Come on!" He pulled the ghoul to the other side of the room.

Verina hissed and jumped. She blocked Harry from the exit. The ghoul screeched and clawed at Verina.

Vincent turned to a mist. He flowed over to Harry. Harry reached into his pocket and threw a handful of metallic dust in Vincent's direction.

The dust hit Vincent, burning him as if he had been hit with a burst of flame. He tried to solidify, but couldn't. Verina sliced at Harry. The ghoul grabbed her arm and pulled it up to her mouth. She ripped a large piece of Verina's flesh away from her body.

Harry pushed past Verina as she clutched her arm. She tried to swipe at the ghoul, but it dived. Vincent concentrated. He separated the dust from himself, then he solidified. The metallic dust settled on the ground.

Verina helped Vincent up. Harry and the ghoul ran out the door. Harry turned around and slammed shut a sliding door that had been hidden in the recess along the entrance. Verina slammed against it as it shut. She jumped back. The places where her skin had touched the door were burnt.

"Fucking ash!" she screamed.

Vincent shook off the last of the burning silver dust. "He's smarter than I gave him credit for."

Verina looked up. She turned to a mist and entered the ventilation. Vincent followed.

Rebecka, he's running. Vincent thought.

Vincent separated from Verina. He found the ducts that connected to the main unit. He flew up them and exited on the roof. He looked over the side. Most of the cars below were covered in snow. The ones that he could see looked like toys.

Vincent stepped off. In seconds he was on the ground. His body slowed down just before impact. Steopa stepped out of the shadows. The darkness followed Steopa for a moment.

"Is he dispatched?" he asked.

Vincent shook his head. "He's armed with ash and silver."

Steopa raised his eyebrow. “Impressive.”

The flashing lights of the snowplow lit where they were standing for a few moments. Vincent turned his attention back to the condo building. Steopa stepped back into the darkness.

Vincent heard a whistle. He turned. Verina and Rebecka were running around the other side of the building. Verina pointed to the entrance while she ran her other hand through her hair. Specks of silver glinted in the light from the street lamps.

Steopa growled. Vincent had started across the plowed street when Harry came out of the building. Harry had his arms around the ghoul, leading her away from the building. He looked around and saw Vincent. Harry paused for a moment, his eyes wide. Vincent heard his heart beat faster. He ran, pulling the ghoul behind him. Steopa and Vincent leaped across the street.

A plow came across a side street. Harry pulled the ghoul in front of the plow. The horn sounded. Vincent stopped. The plow brushed his chest. Something large blurred by him. Steopa jumped over the plow. The snowplow stopped. The tracks still spun. Vincent jumped over the plow as it pulled forward only on one side. Steopa stood at the back of the plow, lifting it up.

Vincent ran on. He caught up with Harry in a few seconds. He grabbed Harry's arm, jerking Harry backwards. His hand that held the ghoul slipped. The ghoul hissed and clawed at Vincent.

Harry pulled something out of his pocket. He swung it with his free hand. Vincent caught it. It burned his hand. Vincent heated up his hand and burned the stake. The tip of it melted, leaving a steaming sliver puddle on the cleared sidewalk.

Vincent misted his hand. His fingertips entered Harry's chest. He stopped when he saw Harry's eyes grow wide, focusing on something behind Vincent. He glanced over his shoulder.

The snowplow flew through the air toward Vincent. He misted just as the machine hit the street and rolled. Harry dived into the loading dock area. The ghoul flattened herself against the ground and slid under the ramp. The plow rolled into the loading area. It crashed through the signs as it slowed its approach. Then it rolled only part way, tilting backward, and rocking to a stop. It blocked the entrance to the street.

Vincent misted through the cab. The plow driver hung by his seat belt, alive and unconscious. Vincent solidified on the other side of the snowplow. He faced the loading dock. Harry had let go of the ghoul. He banged on the delivery door. The ghoul scrambled along the ground, sniffing the air.

Her head snapped up. Vincent could smell blood coming from the plow driver. He had a trickle of blood flowing down his face. She purred. The ghoul ignored Vincent. She tensed, sniffing the air. Harry stopped hammering on the door.

Harry turned around as Vincent grabbed his coat and lifted Harry above his head.

"Missing someone?" Vincent asked.

Harry scratched Vincent's hand. Vincent slapped him. Rebecka jumped down and landed near him on the dock. She raised her claws. Vincent shook his head.

"You have a video camera on that phone?" Vincent asked.

Rebecka nodded. She pulled it out and held it up. Vincent grinned at the camera, then he turned to Harry.

"So now that your gravy train is gone what are you going to do?" he asked.

"Do you need someone?" Harry asked. "I know how to protect your kind. I can bring you food. I can make it so the women come to you," Harry said. "I was the one who found that spell. It works..."

"I suppose you are offering me your assistance out of the kindness of your heart," Vincent said.

Harry's eyes went wild in their sockets. "Man, they are gonna hang me."

"I think this state uses lethal injection. Why did you save that thing?" Vincent motioned with his head, toward the ghoul.

The ghoul had climbed up the side of the plow. She sniffed around the door, growling and purring as she did.

"She's my sister!"

Vincent gagged. How could he let her live like that? Vincent thought.

"What?"

"Nathan took her as one of his victims," Harry said. "He made her a vampire. But she couldn't do it. She couldn't drink human blood. She was a vegetarian!"

Vincent turned his head away so he didn't laugh in Harry's face. "It was her own goddamn fault."

Harry stopped struggling. “I went after him. But he convinced me that I should stay on and help control my sister.”

“So you started to drug his meals. You helped him out, then helped yourself out.”

“He didn't mind,” Harry said. “He couldn't do it anymore. He would sometimes watch.”

“Even after they were dead?”

Harry shrugged. “What do you care? You're dead too.”

It took all of Vincent's strength not to slam Harry's head against the wall and see his brains flow down the bricks. He lowered Harry down and pulled him so they were almost touching noses.

“You know, I don't care how you get your thrills,” Vincent said. “But the police might.”

Harry pushed Vincent. Vincent pinned him against the wall. Harry shook his head. “No, no, no, no.”

“Calling them now,” Rebecka said. She had her phone next to her ear.

Harry hit his head against the bricks. “No, don't call them,” he said. He sobbed. “I have to take care of my sister. Angelica!”

Vincent dropped Harry. He curled up on the concrete crying. Vincent turned around. The ghoul had stopped clawing at the snowplow operator. Her eyes were fixed on Vincent. She tensed her body.

The ghoul hissed and jumped, but Verina moved fast -- so fast that Vincent couldn't follow her. The ghoul hit something in mid-air, spun, and landed on the ground, spraying snow as it rolled to a stop. Verina reappeared. She cleaned her nails as she walked toward Vincent. From underneath the ghoul, blood flowed in a widening pool.

Vincent smiled at Harry. “I don't think that is an issue now.”

The first hint of sirens could be heard in the distance. Rebecka faded into the shadows Vincent squatted down and growled.

“Hurry up, they are coming for him,” Verina said.

He picked Harry up and threw him against the plow. Harry groaned when he hit the snow. The sirens grew louder.

Verina and Vincent left the loading dock and walked down the street. Steopa and Rebecka caught up with them a few moments later. The sidewalks were not cleared yet, and wouldn't be until much later that day. But that did not matter, they walked on top of

the snow.
Three police cars passed them. Vincent walked backwards so he could talk to Steopa.
"I wonder how they are going to explain the snowplow tipping over."
Steopa shrugged. "I am sure they will come up with something."
"You know what I could kill for," Verina said.
"You already killed that ghoul," Vincent said.
"I want a coffee."
Rebecka gagged. Vincent laughed. "I think your taste buds have been ruined by those cigarettes."
"Coffee?" Rebecka asked. "I can't even handle tea."
"I'm craving coffee," Verina said. "Besides, I know a place."
"You always do," Vincent said.
"Rebecka and I will retire," Steopa said.
Steopa and Rebecka could not see, but Verina gave Vincent a little smile.
"Sure," Vincent said. "Hey, come by the club tomorrow."
"You're going back?" Rebecka asked.
"I am so sick of that tomb," Vincent said.
Steopa wrapped his arm around Rebecka. "We have to go."
"See you tomorrow," Rebecka said. She and Steopa disappeared.
Verina hooked her arm in Vincent's. "I really do want a coffee."
"So where are we going?"
Verina smiled, but didn't answer him. She turned to a mist. Vincent followed her.

CHAPTER 17

Verina came back to the table. She set down her large espresso. "I am going to leave for a little while," she said.

"The last time you said that, I didn't see you for over fifty years," Vincent said.

Verina lit a cigarette. "I know, but fifty years flew by."

"I spent most of that time in Forest Grove."

"Why?"

"Nothing much was going on."

"You should have come to Europe with me," Verina said.

"I dunno, Europe? I am such a redneck sometimes."

Verina laughed. "You would have loved England in the sixties and the early seventies. Did I tell you I saw one of the first shows Black Sabbath ever played?"

Another couple squeezed past their table.

"Yes, you did," Vincent said. "But why this time?"

"A few reasons." Verina took two long drags off her cigarette. "It's about your friends."

"John and Lorelei?"

"No, Steopa and Rebecka. There are rumors I am pretty sure are about him."

"What about?"

Verina waved her hand. "It's nothing."

"You have peaked my interest. You were right, he did kill the vampire that made him. While she was feeding on him."

"Are you sure?"

"Yes."

"It would be best if he stayed in America."

"Verina, be straight with me," Vincent said.

She sipped her coffee. "They are linked. Personally I think it's charming, but there are other vampires that would not like it."

"I saw. Some of the ones that came tonight. The older one, she didn't looked please."

Verina nodded. "I like coming to America. Most of the vampires here do not have to ask permission just to be. The ones in Europe have rules. Steopa broke most of them."

"So what? He's got some vampires looking for him?"

Verina shrugged. "Not some, many."

"So what would their opinion be of me?" Vincent asked.

"What would they think of you?" Verina sat back in her chair. A small smile formed on her face. "You would scare them."

Vincent scoffed.

"Seriously. You were not made by another vampire, they would not know how to deal with you."

"Like it matters."

"It would with some. But those are the ones that still cringe when they see the cross."

"Crosses never bothered me."

"Nor I, but then I was already..." Verina reached over and took Vincent's hand. "I also lied to you earlier. I was not with anyone else when I was attacked by those crusaders."

"What do you mean?"
Verina pointed to the necklace. "That used to be mine, along with the ring and the bracelet. I am not upset the bracelet is gone. And I am happy you have the necklace."
"How did you get them?"
"I'd rather not say."
Vincent saw for a moment Verina's age appear. Her outward appearance did not change, but her eyes gave him the impression of someone who had seen the world for centuries and what she had seen tired her.
"Are they dangerous?" Vincent asked.
"If you know how to use them, no. But too many would want their powers and abuse them. Wear it well."
"Maybe you could show me-"
"I don't want to touch it," Verina said. She picked up her handbag.
"How did you lose them?" Vincent asked.
"I didn't, but the people I asked to watch over them were murdered."
"When?"
"1941." Verina adjusted her purse strap over her shoulder. "We are lucky no one in power at the time knew about those."
"You have to tell me more," Vincent said. He took Verina's hand.
She looked away. "It was nice seeing you again."
"Next time, don't wait fifty years," Vincent said.
Verina nodded and left the coffee shop. Vincent sat for a few minutes, then he walked back to the Rathskeller just as the sky started to turn gray because of dawn approaching. The building was quiet. Everyone who lived in the building was asleep. He found a note pinned to his door from Andi. Vincent pulled it off and went into his apartment.
He read the note. Andi had to speak to him. He went into his bedroom and laid down on the mattress.
"I never want to spend another night in a crypt," he said. Dawn broke over the horizon and Vincent went to the stupor, smiling.
Night came and the Rathskeller hadn't opened yet when Vincent walked into the bouncer cage. Swen came in a few moments later. He took off his leather jacket and sat down.
"Is Cassie all right? You know, about..." Vincent asked.

"It broke her heart," Swen said. "Mine too."
"What about-?"
"We've been through all the options. Maybe in a few years we will adopt, but..."
"But?"
"It is the end of my family line. I'm an only child and my uncle never had kids."
"That's a bummer."
"Yeah." Swen turned on the small TV that hung above the cage. Vincent leaned against the counter and didn't pay attention to the screen until the news came on.
"Disturbing news today. Nathan Stout, the author of the *Ashes* series of books, is missing and his business partner has been arrested on multiple counts of murder," the announcer said.
The news cut to a fan with tears in her eyes. "It's unreal. I was at his book signing a little while back."
"Harry Jones, Mr. Stout's business manager, had been picked up by the police after he was involved in a freak accident. The police searched the condo that Jones and Stout owned and found human remains."
Grady appeared on the screen. "We contacted other law enforcement offices across the country. Mr. Jones is suspected in the murder of at least fifteen people."
"Nathan Stout is missing. The last person to see him was the doorman at the building. Right now, Mr. Stout is only considered a missing person. It is not known if he was an accomplice to the multiple murders."
Vincent covered his mouth and laughed. "He is under about six inches of snow now."
"Did that guy do all that?" Swen asked.
"He didn't kill them, or eat them, he just had his own fun."
"Sick bastard."
"The freak accident that injured Harry Jones, happened at 2 a.m. this morning, involving snow plow driver Earl Jenkins," the news reporter said.
The news cut to the snow plow driver with a bandaged nose. "It was the weirdest thing. The plow was moving along then it was like I was lifted into the air, and it rolled."
The reporter pointed to the condo. "The plow rolled into the

loading dock area of this building, where Harry Jones was found. If it hadn't been for the plow blocking his escape, the police would not have made that grisly discovery."

"What really happened?" Swen asked.

"Steopa rolled it."

"Was it a truck or a grader?"

"A grader."

"Damn." Swen whistled.

Chuck and Andi walked in through the back door. Swen swung his legs off the counter and stood up. "Socializing tonight?" he asked.

Andi didn't look like her normal self. She wore a simple black dress and none of her outrageous makeup. "We just got back from Janice's funeral," she said. "Vincent, can I talk to you?"

Vincent nodded. He left the cage. Andi pulled Vincent back to his private room. When they got inside, Andi turned around.

"Chuck and I want to get married," she said.

The word "married" jumped around his head for a moment, then Vincent's mouth dropped open. "Wait, you've only known him for a few weeks."

"My mom and dad only knew each other for two days."

"This isn't because you are grieving, is it?"

Andi shook her head. "No, I really like Chuck."

"I think you are supposed to say love."

She opened her mouth, then shut it. She shrugged. "I know."

"You don't mind? That he is a werewolf?"

Andi scoffed. "I work with a vampire and a berserk. You think a werewolf would scare me?"

Vincent sat down. "So you want to marry a werewolf you hardly know?"

"Yes." Andi sat down next to him.

"I am not telling you not to-"

"Like I would listen to you anyway."

"When is the wedding?"

"We haven't set a date," she said. "At least a year from now. See? We weren't going to jump into it right away."

"Good," Vincent said. "I've seen too many rushed marriages end up bad."

"Well, that's one reason, and the other is that he can only marry another werewolf."

"But you're not... I see," Vincent said. "You want to become a werewolf? Are you sure?"

"It's not like with you. You know, like what happened with Rebecka. I guess he could just bite me, but then he might not stop."

"That would put a damper on your relationship."

Andi slugged him, but she put no power into it. Vincent rubbed his arm, even though it did not hurt.

"Ow."

"You deserved it."

"Okay, but what about the rest of his family?"

"The ones I met, I like. I know his dad likes me. When Chuck called him yesterday to tell him the news, he talked to me for over an hour to make sure I knew what I was getting into."

"Are you sure you want to?"

"Chuck has told me what will be done to me," she said, her voice softer. "I want you to be there."

Vincent could not answer. He thought that werewolves only had to bite a human to make them a werewolf. But then the same myth existed about vampires. If all it took was a bite, the world would be covered by vampires and werewolves.

But she had invited him to something. There were so many things you could invite him to: birthday parties, bachelor parties, watching the Super Bowl, or even a baptism. Was she talking about ending her life as a human?

Andi waited for him to respond.

"What are you talking about?" he asked.

"From what Chuck told me, there are few ways to become a werewolf," Andi said. "Most aren't nice. The one he suggested is like a ceremony. It's the only way that his family would let me in."

"So it's just a ceremony?"

"Ah, yeah." She looked away from Vincent.

"Andi?"

"Well, it's a little drawn out. His father went over it with me last night, just to make sure I understood."

"What type of ceremony?"

Andi sighed, "It's just a little ritual. Chuck's family has a place out in the country where they do it. I can invite people to watch. And I thought you might find it interesting."

"When is it?"

"In the spring." Andi took his hand. "Don't be upset."

Vincent shook his head. "I'm not upset."

"I won't be able to have you feed from me anymore."

Vincent nodded. "I thought as much. You know I tried to drink Swen's blood before."

"What happened?"

"I don't remember much. I drank from his wrist, then crashed through a wall. Woke up in the freezer. I had ripped the walls apart."

Andi giggled. "Wow."

"Lorelei almost staked me for that."

"From what Steopa told me, you could still drink my blood. You could get sick, though."

"Steopa told you that?"

Andi nodded.

"But I would not flip out."

"I still don't think it would be a good idea."

"Too bad."

Vincent pulled his hand away, but then brushed her hair away from her cheek. With John and Lorelei, the blood he took was a business arrangement. With Andi it had always been a little fun. Feeding off Andi was like eating a rich dessert when all you had to eat before was bread. She was something to be savored.

"I think that would be best, yes," Vincent said. "I don't like the idea of Chuck standing outside the door."

"Thanks Vincent." She leaned over and kissed his forehead. "There was a time I wanted to ask you to turn me into a vampire."

Vincent tried not to smirk, but it happened. "It wouldn't have worked. I can't do it."

"You won't?"

"I can't."

Andi stood up and frowned. "Don't worry. It was a stupid idea of mine."

She turned to leave.

"One more thing," Vincent said.

Andi turned around.

"You realize that you will be eating a lot of meat from now on," Vincent said, giving her a wink.

"I know. It's gonna piss off my vegan girlfriends."

CHAPTER 18

Months passed. The nights had started to get shorter and the weather warmer. Vincent could smell that the trees were almost ready to bud. Flowers had started to bloom. He stood outside the Rathskeller and glanced at the invitation in his hand one more time.

Tonight, Andi would change. She would no longer be human when the sun rose.

She had arranged for Vincent to be picked up by one of the members of Chuck's family. Vincent watched the people walking up and down the street. A few of the braver ones were walking without jackets. In a few hours it would be cold enough to see your breath, but not now.

Vincent felt Steopa and Rebecka approaching. He looked up and down the street trying to find them. A minivan pulled up in front of him. He saw the unmistakable shape of Steopa in the back. Vincent walked up to the van. The driver rolled down the passenger window. A dark-haired man leaned over the front seat. His close-shaved dark beard accented his smile. His spiked hair cut looked like it had been messed up, but that was the style.

"Vincent?" he called out.

Vincent nodded.

"Get in." He waved Vincent over.

Vincent walked to the passenger side. He waved to Steopa and Rebecka sitting in the back seat. "What are you doing here?" he asked.

"Andi invited me," Rebecka said, "and Steopa is a friend of Chuck's family."

"Cool," Vincent said.

The driver held out his hand. "Teodor Navarro. Just call me Teodor," he said. "Chuck's dad."

Vincent shook his hand. Teodor and Chuck looked about the same age.

"His dad?" Vincent asked. "But you look like his brother."

Teodor laughed. "We stop aging in our late twenties."

"How old are you?"

"Old."

As they left downtown, Vincent began to recognize parts of the city. Once in a while he would see a familiar landmark. But the city and surrounding area had changed. Suburbs had taken the place of the rolling farmland and the forests that Vincent remembered.

"Where are we going?" Vincent asked.

"A little plot of land my family bought for events like these," Teodor said. "You really can't do this ceremony in the middle of the city. Well, you could, but it wouldn't feel right, you know?"

The suburbs started to thin out. The grids of lights began to fill with more black. Steopa leaned forward and said something to Teodor in a language that Vincent did not recognize.

Teodor responded in the same language. Vincent looked over his shoulder to Rebecka, she shrugged.

"Don't worry," Teodor said to Steopa. "This is not the same ceremony that my father insisted on using."

"Of course, you cannot get prisoners like he could," Steopa said.

Teodor caught Vincent's eye. "My father was very traditional. The best thing that happened to him was the Civil War."

"What happened?" Vincent asked.

"The soldiers raided my family's estate and killed them. They were hunted down with silver bullets and burned."

"Ah," Vincent said. "I see, you did not get along with your family."

"I was the runt," Teodor said.

"How did you get away?"

"The villagers liked me, because I never tried to eat them. They hid me until the rest of my family was destroyed."

Teodor pulled off the freeway. The road they were on curved and twisted as he drove them further out into the country. Vincent rolled down the window and smelled the night air. It did not have the mess of odors that the city air had. But the country air had its own intensity.

"*Ashes at Dawn* is a flop," Rebecka said. "Steopa and I saw it last night. You could tell they hurried to get it out. It felt like I was watching a bad soap opera. The club looked good though."

"I did like the vampire hunter," Steopa said. "I would have read the books if he had been the main character."

"Why?" Vincent asked.

"Because he was honorable."

Vincent turned in his seat. "Did you know Nathan had put a thrall in the actual writing?"

Rebecka nodded. "Ogden told us. You should see the repercussions. Go online. Almost all his former fans are trashing the stories. Except the ones who put up memorials to him."

"I would think that being listed as a victim of a serial killer helped with that," Teodor said. Then he added with a large smirk on his face. "I take it his body was never found."

"And will never be," Vincent said.

"Is it true you burned him?"

Vincent nodded. Teodor laughed. Vincent looked out the

window and recognized the bar and church they drove by. He had been out here when he had been a child. The forests were larger, some of the buildings were newer, but not much else had changed.

Teodor pulled onto a dirt road. The trees crowded the road. Vincent could see a bonfire ahead. A couple hundred yards later, the road ended in a clearing. There were other cars parked along one side of the bonfire. A truck had its tailgate down with coolers of food and drinks. Vincent noticed all the meat was raw.

Teodor parked. He nodded to the small group of people outside. "My kids."

Everyone outside of the van looked to be in their mid-twenties. Only two women were in the group; one was Andi. The other woman stood between Andi and a lanky young man. She laughed, her wavy dark hair blew across her face. She looked like Teodor, as did most of the men. The only one that did not was the lanky one.

As Vincent got out of the van he realized the other young men were two sets of twins. He waved to Chuck. Chuck waved back, then turned to his twin. The sets of twins were fraternal; each set had a dark-haired and a light-haired twin.

Steopa emerged from the back of the van. One of the young men lifted a beer can. "Steopa!"

Rebecka climbed out. She chuckled. "They call him uncle sometimes."

"How long have you known them?" Vincent asked.

"Since I changed. Steopa and Teodor have a long history."

"Do you know what's going to happen?"

Rebecka shook her head. "All Steopa told me is that it's not as brutal as the old way."

Teodor waved Rebecka and Vincent over. "Let me introduce you."

The sets of twins were Chuck and Jamie, and Bill and Nick. Nick had the blond hair, as did Chuck. Jamie and Bill shared their father's black hair. Seeing all of them together was like looking at photocopies of a single person.

"This is Trucker, my son-in-law, if you will," Teodor said. He pointed to the lanky man.

Trucker pushed up his wire-rim glasses then shook Vincent's hand.

"My daughter, Silvia. Soon she won't be the only female."

She didn't shake Vincent's hand, but she did smile. Then she turned to Andi. “It's time.”

Teodor nodded. “Yeah, almost ready. Trucker, did you bring it?”

“Yeah,” Trucker said.

He opened the door on the car next to him. He pulled out a small carved wood case. Vincent could not make out any of the carvings in the firelight.

Silvia took Andi's hand and they walked off into the woods. Vincent and Rebecka joined Steopa as the rest of the family began to gather around the bonfire.

“Have you ever seen this?” Vincent asked Steopa.

“No, Teodor told me about it.”

Bill placed a wooden TV tray next to the fire. Trucker laid the case on it. Teodor opened the case part way. He nodded, then shut it. Nick stood a little away from the rest of them. He had a few small bottles on the hood of a car. He held one up to the fire, read its label, then poured its contents into a large stein.

The rest formed a semi-circle around the flames. The vampires joined the semi-circle, but stayed near each other. Teodor patted the case.

“For our friends here, I am going to give you a bit of history,” he said. “There are as many ways to become one of our kind as there are ways to become a vampire. All my children were born werewolves. Family is very important to us. And it is a happy day that someone wants to join our family, even when they know that they will have to give up being human.”

Teodor ran his fingers over the case while he spoke. “In the old days, there were shamans and other holy people that could join us, for a short time. Their secrets have unfortunately died with them.” Teodor paused, and cleared his throat. “Then in later years, when the packs were hunted, other ways were developed. Trucker has already taken the path and become one of us. Tonight we welcome a new member to our pack.”

Silvia returned with Andi. Andi had changed into a deep red bathrobe. She stumbled as she walked toward the fire. Silvia steadied her. Vincent saw Andi's bare feet under the robe. Andi paused. She lifted one foot up and pulled out a small stick that had embedded itself in her foot. She glanced at Vincent and mouthed “Ouch.”

Teodor continued. “The method Andi has chosen is an old method. A method that was almost lost when the more violent ways were chosen.”

He opened the case. He pulled out a wolf's skin. Teodor ran his hand over the pelt. He sniffed. “My children remember their mother fondly. She gave her life trying to protect them.”

Teodor coughed, he turned his head. When he turned back, the firelight reflected in his watery eyes. “But she left us a great gift.”

Chuck came up to Teodor. He pulled a knife from his boot. Teodor stepped back. Chuck stroked the pelt.

“Mom, thank you,” he said.

He sliced a strip of hide a few inches thick off of it. Teodor folded the pelt and placed it back into the case. Chuck held the strip up.

Teodor turned to Andi. “Are you sure you want to join our pack?”

Andi glanced over at Vincent, then she nodded. Chuck came over to Andi, still holding the strip of pelt. She dropped her robe. Vincent rubbed his goatee. He glanced around the semi-circle, no one seemed embarrassed that Andi stood in front of them, nude.

Chuck wrapped the strip around her waist, tying it at the front. He kissed her lips, then stepped back. Teodor laid his hand on Andi's shoulder and whispered to her. When he finished, Nick came over to the fire carrying the stein. He handed it to Andi.

Steopa leaned over to Vincent. “Now we will see if she can make the transition.”

Steopa stepped away before Vincent could ask what he meant. Andi raised the cup. She paused, a few inches from her lips. She sighed, then took a sip.

Vincent smelled the mixture of herbs and drugs. Opium, hemlock, and a plant he could not identify were mixed in a wine. Vincent closed his eyes for a moment. This is what Andi didn't want to tell him. The hemlock would kill her.

He opened his eyes.

Andi lowered the stein. She coughed. She glanced up at Chuck, who laid his hand on her arm. Andi raised the stein again. She drank the rest of the mixture like she was chugging a beer. She lowered the stein again, and wiped her face. The stein dropped from her fingers. Andi fell to her knees and threw up. Teodor and

Chuck stepped back, but did not assist her in any way.

Vincent moved forward. Steopa placed his large hand on Vincent's shoulder. “Do not,” he whispered.

Andi doubled over, clutching her stomach. She rolled on the ground, moaning, then crying. Chuck took a step toward her, only to be pulled back by Teodor.

Vincent heard Andi's heart beat faster. Then it began to skip beats. Andi rolled on her back and screamed. Her body twisted into a stiff arch. She held her body in that position, like she was trying to buck off the sky above her, for a moment. Then she collapsed. Vincent could no longer hear her heartbeat.

There were no sounds in the clearing. No owls hooted, the wind didn't blow, and no one, even if they were capable, breathed. A single thump, then another. Andi's heart started to beat again. She drew in a deep breath.

The belt disappeared, fading into her skin. Andi rolled onto her side. She held her hand out to Chuck, who helped her stand. As she stood up, the belt could no longer be seen. Chuck picked up the robe from the ground and wrapped it around her. Andi's eyes were unfocused. She giggled.

Andi leaned on Chuck as they walked back to the cars. Chuck took her to the large van. He opened the back door. A mattress had been laid on the floor. Chuck helped her inside. She fell onto the bed. He shut the door.

“We'll let her sleep for a while,” Chuck said.

“Anyone want some food?” Silvia asked.

Teodor's family gathered around the truck, laughing and joking as if this had been a picnic. Vincent, Steopa, and Rebecka stayed where they were.

“She's going to be all right, isn't she?” Vincent asked.

Steopa nodded. “She survived.”

Vincent watched the gathering around the trunk of the car. Silvia threw a piece of meat at Jamie, who caught it with his mouth. Trucker and Nick opened a couple of beers. They leaned against the truck and had an animated conversation.

Vincent glanced at Steopa and Rebecka. They stood with their arms around each other, turned inward, so their bodies were touching. Rebecka leaned on Steopa, resting her head against his chest.

“Amazing what some people will do for love,” Vincent said.

Steopa wrapped Rebecka in his arms. “Can you call what we feel love?”

Vincent shrugged. “Why? Because it's too human?”

“Yes.”

“Then what about you two?”

“What about you and Verina?” Rebecka asked.

“She's a friend.”

Rebecka giggled. “I think love is too soft of a word.”

Chuck came over, chewing on a strip of meat. He had two beers in his hand. “Thanks for coming. Dad tells me not many vampires have seen this.”

“It was... interesting,” Vincent said.

Chuck handed Vincent a beer. “I know it's not blood, but I feel we need to toast this night.”

Vincent took the bottle and twisted off the cap.

“To Andi,” he said.

Chuck raised his bottle. “To Andi.”

Vincent sipped the beer. Chuck turned around and went back to his family. Vincent spit the beer out. Steopa chuckled.

“That is why I stick with vodka. No taste,” Steopa said.

Vincent dumped the rest of the beer out. “I suppose in Europe something like this would not happen.”

Steopa nodded. “Vampires and werewolves are kept apart there.”

“Too bad.” Vincent fingered the necklace. Things were changing, he could feel that. He smiled.

About the Author

Mari Miniatt lives in Syracuse, NY with her husband, sons, and two cats. You can find her either at work, or writing in the coffee shops.

7023148R0

Made in the USA
Charleston, SC
11 January 2011